THE TOWER TREASURE

Joe toppled over the railing into space!

Hardy Boys Mystery Stories

THE TOWER
TREASURE

BY

FRANKLIN W. DIXON

NEW YORK
GROSSET & DUNLAP
A NATIONAL GENERAL COMPANY
Publishers

ISBN: 0–448–08901–7 (TRADE EDITION)
ISBN: 0–448–18901–1 (LIBRARY EDITION)

*In this new story, based on the original of
the same title, Mr. Dixon has incorporated
the most up-to-date methods used by police
and private detectives.*

CONTENTS

THE TOWER TREASURE

CHAPTER I

The Speed Demon

FRANK and Joe Hardy clutched the grips of their motorcycles and stared in horror at the oncoming car. It was careening from side to side on the narrow road.

"He'll hit us! We'd better climb this hillside—and fast!" Frank exclaimed, as the boys brought their motorcycles to a screeching halt and leaped off.

"On the double!" Joe cried out as they started up the steep embankment.

To their amazement, the reckless driver suddenly pulled his car hard to the right and turned into a side road on two wheels. The boys expected the car to turn over, but it held the dusty ground and sped off out of sight.

"Wow!" said Joe. "Let's get away from here before the crazy guy comes back. That's a dead-end road, you know."

The boys scrambled back onto their motorcycles and gunned them a bit to get past the intersecting road in a hurry. They rode in silence for a while, gazing at the scene ahead.

On their right an embankment of tumbled rocks and boulders sloped steeply to the water below. From the opposite side rose a jagged cliff. The little-traveled road was winding, and just wide enough for two cars to pass.

"Boy, I'd hate to fall off the edge of this road," Frank remarked. "It's a hundred-foot drop."

"That's right," Joe agreed. "We'd sure be smashed to bits before we ever got to the bottom." Then he smiled. "Watch your step, Frank, or Dad's papers won't get delivered."

Frank reached into his jacket pocket to be sure several important legal papers which he was to deliver for Mr. Hardy were still there. Relieved to find them, Frank chuckled and said, "After the help we gave Dad on his latest case, he ought to set up the firm of Hardy and Sons."

"Why not?" Joe replied with a broad grin. "Isn't he one of the most famous private detectives in the country? And aren't we bright too?" Then, becoming serious, he added, "I wish we could solve a mystery on our own, though."

Frank and Joe, students at Bayport High, were combining business with pleasure this Saturday morning by doing the errand for their father.

Even though one boy was dark and the other

fair, there was a marked resemblance between the two brothers. Eighteen-year-old Frank was tall and dark. Joe, a year younger, was blond with blue eyes. They were the only children of Fenton and Laura Hardy. The family lived in Bayport, a small but thriving city of fifty thousand inhabitants, located on Barmet Bay, three miles inland from the Atlantic Ocean.

The two motorcycles whipped along the narrow road that skirted the bay and led to Willowville, the brothers' destination. The boys took the next curve neatly and started up a long, steep slope. Here the road was a mere ribbon and badly in need of repair.

"Once we get to the top of the hill it won't be so rough," Frank remarked, as they jounced over the uneven surface. "Better road from there into Willowville."

Just then, above the sharp put-put of their own motors, the two boys heard the roar of a car approaching from their rear at great speed. They took a moment to glance back.

"Looks like that same guy we saw before!" Joe burst out. "Good night!"

At once the Hardys stopped and pulled as close to the edge as they dared. Frank and Joe hopped off and stood poised to leap out of danger again if necessary.

The car hurtled toward them like a shot. Just when it seemed as if it could not miss them, the driver swung the wheel about viciously and the sedan sped past.

"Whew! That was close!" Frank gasped.

The car had been traveling at such high speed that the boys had been unable to get the license number or a glimpse of the driver's features. But they had noted that he was hatless and had a shock of red hair.

"If I ever meet him again," Joe muttered, "I'll —I'll—" The boy was too excited to finish the threat.

Frank relaxed. "He must be practicing for some kind of race," he remarked, as the dark-blue sedan disappeared from sight around the curve ahead.

The boys resumed their journey. By the time

they rounded the curve, and could see Willowville in a valley along the bay beneath them, there was no trace of the rash motorist.

"He's probably halfway across the state by this time," Joe remarked.

"Unless he's in jail or over a cliff," Frank added.

The boys reached Willowville and Frank delivered the legal papers to a lawyer while Joe guarded the motorcycles. When his brother returned, Joe suggested, "How about taking the other road back to Bayport? I don't crave going over that bumpy stretch again."

"Suits me. We can stop off at Chet's."

Chet Morton, who was a school chum of the Hardy boys, lived on a farm about a mile out of Bayport. The pride of Chet's life was a bright yellow jalopy which he had named Queen. He worked on it daily to "soup up" the engine.

Frank and Joe retraced their trip for a few miles, then turned onto a country road which led to the main highway on which the Morton farm was situated. As they neared Chet's home, Frank suddenly brought his motorcycle to a stop and peered down into a clump of bushes in a deep ditch at the side of the road.

"Joe! That crazy driver or somebody else had a crack-up!"

Among the tall bushes was an overturned blue sedan. The car was a total wreck, and lay wheels upward, a mass of tangled junk.

"We'd better see if there's anyone underneath," Joe cried out.

The boys made their way down the culvert, their hearts pounding. What would they find?

A close look into the sedan and in the immediate vicinity proved that there was no victim around.

"Maybe this happened some time ago," said Joe, "and—"

Frank stepped forward and laid his hand on the exposed engine. "Joe, it's still warm," he said. "The accident occurred a short while ago. Now

I'm sure this is the red-haired driver's car."

"But what about him?" Joe asked. "Is he alive? Did somebody rescue him, or what happened?"

Frank shrugged. "One thing I *can* tell you. Either he or somebody else removed the license plates to avoid identification."

The brothers were completely puzzled by the whole affair. Since their assistance was not needed at the spot, they climbed out of the culvert and back onto their motorcycles. Before long they were in sight of the Mortons' home, a rambling old farmhouse with an apple orchard at the rear. When they drove up the lane they saw Chet at the barnyard gate.

"Hi, fella!" Joe called.

Chet hurried down the lane to meet them. He was a plump boy who loved to eat and was rarely without an apple or a pocket of cookies. His round, freckled face usually wore a smile. But today the Hardys sensed something was wrong. As they brought their motorcycles to a stop, they noticed that their chum's cheery expression was missing.

"What's the matter?" Frank asked.

"I'm in trouble," Chet replied. "You're just in time to help me. Did you meet a fellow driving the Queen?"

Frank and Joe looked at each other blankly.

"Your car? No, we haven't seen it," said Joe. "What's happened?"

"It's been stolen!"

"Stolen!"

"Yes. I just came out to the garage to get the Queen and she was gone," Chet answered mournfully.

"Wasn't the car locked?"

"That's the strange part of it. She was locked, although the garage door was open. I can't see how anyone got away with it."

"A professional job," Frank commented. "Auto thieves always carry scores of keys with them. Chet, have you any idea when this happened?"

"Not more than fifteen minutes ago, because that's when I came home with the car."

"We're wasting time!" Joe cried out. "Let's chase that thief!"

"But I don't know which way he went," Chet protested.

"We didn't meet him, so he must have gone in the other direction," Frank reasoned.

"Climb on behind me, Chet," Joe urged. "The Queen can't go as fast as our motorcycles. We'll catch her in no time!"

"And there was only a little gas in my car, anyway," Chet said excitedly as he swung himself onto Joe's motorcycle. "Maybe it has stalled by this time."

In a few moments the boys were tearing down the road in pursuit of the automobile thief!

CHAPTER II

The Holdup

CHET MORTON's jalopy was such a brilliant yellow that the boys were confident it would not be difficult to pick up the trail of the auto thief.

"The Queen's pretty well known around Bayport," Frank remarked. "We should meet someone who saw it."

"Seems strange to me," said Joe, "that a thief would take a car like that. Auto thieves usually take cars of a standard make and color. They're easier to get rid of."

"It's possible," Frank suggested, "that the thief didn't steal the car to sell it. Maybe, for some reason, he was making a fast getaway and he'll abandon it."

"Look!" Chet exclaimed, pointing to a truck garden where several men were hoeing cabbage plants. "Maybe they saw the Queen."

"I'll ask them," Frank offered, and brought his motorcycle to a stop.

9

He scrambled over the fence and jumped across the rows of small plants until he reached the first farm hand.

"Did you see a yellow jalopy go by here within the past hour?" Frank asked him.

The lanky old farmer leaned on his hoe and put a hand to one ear. "Eh?" he shouted.

"Did you see a fellow pass along here in a bright yellow car?" Frank repeated in a louder tone.

The farmer called to his companions. As they ambled over, the old man removed a plug of tobacco from the pocket of his overalls and took a hearty chew.

"Lad here wants to know if we saw a jalopy come by," he said slowly.

The other three farm hands, all rather elderly men, did not answer at once. Instead, they laid down their hoes and the plug of tobacco was duly passed around the group.

Frank grit his teeth. "Please hurry up and answer. The car was stolen. We're trying to find the thief!"

"That so?" said one of the men. "A hot rod, eh?"

"Yes. A bright yellow one," Frank replied.

Another of the workers removed his hat and mopped his brow. "Seems to me," he drawled, "I did see a car come by here a while ago."

"A yellow car?"

"No—'twarn't yeller, come to think of it. I guess,

anyhow, it was a delivery truck, if I remember rightly."

Frank strove to conceal his impatience. "Please, did any of you—?"

"Was it a brand-new car, real shiny?" asked the fourth member of the group.

"No, it was an old car, but it was painted bright yellow," Frank explained.

"My nephew had one of them things," the farmer remarked. "Never thought they was safe, myself."

"I don't agree with you," still another man spoke up. "All boys like cars and you might as well let 'em have one they can work on themselves."

"You're all wrong!" the deaf man interrupted. "Let the boys work on the farm truck. That way they won't get into mischief!" He gave a cackling sort of laugh. "Well, son, I guess we ain't been much help to you. Hope you find the critter that stole your hot rod."

"Thanks," said Frank, and joined the other boys. "No luck. Let's go!"

As they approached Bayport, the trio saw a girl walking along the road ahead of them. When the cyclists drew nearer, Frank's face lighted up, for he had recognized Callie Shaw, who was in his class at Bayport High. Frank often dated Callie and liked her better than any girl he knew.

The boys brought their motorcycles to a stop

beside pretty, brown-eyed Callie. Under one arm she was carrying a slightly battered package. She looked vexed.

"Hi, Callie! What's the matter?" Frank asked. "You look as if your last friend had gone off in a moon rocket."

Callie gave a mischievous smile. "How could I think that with you three friends showing up? Or are you about to take off?" Then her smile faded and she held out the damaged package. "Look at that!" she exclaimed. "It's your fault, Chet Morton!"

The stout boy gulped. "M-my fault? How do you figure that?"

"Well, dear old Mrs. Wills down the road is ill, so I baked her a cake."

"Lucky Mrs. Wills," Joe broke in. "Callie, I'm feeling terribly ill."

Callie ignored him. "That man in the car came along here so fast that I jumped to the side of the road and dropped my package. I'm afraid my cake is ruined!"

"What man?" Joe asked.

"The one Chet lent his car to."

"Callie, that's the man we're looking for!" Frank exclaimed. "Chet didn't lend him the car. He stole it!"

"Oh!" said Callie, shocked. "Chet, that's a shame."

"Was he heading for Bayport?" Joe asked.

"Yes, and at the speed he was making the poor Queen travel, you'll never catch him."

Chet groaned. "I just remembered that the gas gauge wasn't working. I guess the car had more gas in it than I thought. No telling where that guy may take my Queen."

"We'd better go to police headquarters," Frank suggested. "Callie, will you describe this man?"

"All I saw," she answered, "was a blur, but the man did have red hair."

"Red hair!" Frank fairly shouted. "Joe, do you think he could be the same man we saw? The one who wrecked his own car?"

Joe wagged his head. "Miracles do happen. Maybe he wasn't hurt very much and walked to Chet's house."

"And helped himself to my car!" Chet added.

Frank snapped his fingers. "Say! Maybe the wrecked car *didn't* belong to that fellow—"

"You mean he'd stolen it, too!" Joe interrupted.

"Yes—which would make him even more desperate to get away."

"Whatever are you boys talking about?" Callie asked.

"I'll phone you tonight and tell you," Frank promised. "Got to dash now."

The boys waved good-by to Callie and hurried into town. They went at once to Chief Ezra Collig, head of the Bayport police force. He was a tall, husky man, well known to Fenton Hardy and his two sons. The chief had often turned to the private detective for help in solving particularly difficult cases.

When the boys went into his office they found the police chief talking with three excited men. One of these was Ike Harrity, the old ticket seller at the city ferryboat office. Another was Policeman Con Riley. The third was Oscar Smuff, a short, stout man. He was invariably seen wearing a checkered suit and a soft felt hat. He called himself a private detective and was working hard to earn a place on the Bayport police force.

"Smuff's playing up to Collig again," Joe whispered, chuckling, as the boys waited for the chief to speak to them.

Ike Harrity was frankly frightened. He was a timid man, who had perched on a high stool behind the ticket window at the ferryboat office day in and day out for a good many years.

"I was just countin' up the mornin's receipts," he was saying in a high-pitched, excited voice, "when in comes this fellow and sticks a revolver in front of my nose."

"Just a minute," interrupted Chief Collig, turning to the newcomers. "What can I do for you boys?"

"I came to report a theft," Chet spoke up. "My hot rod has been stolen."

"Why, it was one of those crazy hot rods this

fellow drove!" Ike Harrity cried out. "A yellow one!"

"Ha!" exclaimed Oscar Smuff. "A clue!" He immediately pulled a pencil and notebook from his pocket.

"My Queen!" shouted Chet.

Chief Collig rapped on his desk for quiet and asked, "What's a queen got to do with all this?"

Chet explained, then the chief related Harrity's story for him.

"A man drove up to the ferryboat office and tried to hold up Mr. Harrity. But a passenger came into the office and the fellow ran away."

As the officer paused, Frank gave Chief Collig a brief account of the wrecked blue sedan near the Morton farm.

"I'll send some men out there right now." The chief pressed a buzzer and quickly relayed his orders.

"It certainly looks," Joe commented, "as if the man who stole Chet's car and the fellow who tried to hold up the ferryboat office are the same person!"

"Did you notice the color of the man's hair?" Frank asked Mr. Harrity.

Smuff interrupted. "What's that got to do with it?"

"It may have a great deal to do with it," Frank replied. "What was the color of his hair, Mr. Harrity?"

"Dark brown and short cropped."

Frank and Joe looked at each other, perplexed. "You're sure it wasn't red?" Joe asked.

Chief Collig sat forward in his chair. "What are you driving at, boys? Have you some information about this man?"

"We were told," said Joe, "that the guy who stole Chet's car had red hair. A friend of ours saw him."

"Then he must have turned the jalopy over to someone else," Chief Collig concluded.

At this moment a short, nervous little man was ushered into the room. He was the passenger who had gone into the ferryboat office at the time of the attempted holdup. Chief Collig had sent for him.

The newcomer introduced himself as Henry J. Brown of New York. He told of entering the office and seeing a man run away from the ticket window with a revolver in his hand.

"What color was his hair?" Frank asked eagerly. "Did you notice?"

"I can't say I did," the man replied. "My eyes were focused on that gun. Say, wait a minute! He had red hair. You couldn't miss it! I noticed it after he jumped into the car."

Oscar Smuff looked bewildered. "You say he had red hair." The detective turned to Mr. Harrity. "And you say he had dark hair. Somethin' wrong somewhere!" He shook his head in puzzlement.

The others were puzzled too. Frank asked Mr. Brown to tell once more just when he had noticed the red hair.

"After the fellow leaned down in the car and popped his head up again," the New Yorker replied.

Frank and Joe exchanged glances. Was it possible the red hair was a wig and the thief had put it on just before Mr. Brown had noticed him? The boys kept still—they didn't want any interference from Smuff in tracking down this clue.

Harrity and Brown began to argue over the color of the thief's hair. Finally Chief Collig had to rap once more for order. "I'll send out an alarm for both this holdup man and for Chet's car. I guess that's all that can be done now."

Undaunted by their failure to catch the thief, the Hardy boys left police headquarters with Chet Morton. They were determined to pursue the case.

"We'll talk with Dad tonight, Chet," Frank promised. "Maybe he'll give us some leads."

"I sure hope so, fellows," their friend replied as they climbed onto the motorcycles.

The same thought was running through Frank's and Joe's minds: maybe this mystery would turn out to be their first case!

CHAPTER III

The Threat

"You're getting to be pretty good on that motorcycle, Frank," Joe said as the boys rode into the Hardy garage. "I'm not even scared to ride alongside you any more!"

"*You're* not scared!" Frank pretended to take Joe seriously. "What about me—riding with a daredevil like you?"

"Well," Joe countered, "let's just admit that we're both pretty good!"

"It sure was swell of Dad to let us have them," Joe continued.

"Yes," Frank agreed. "And if we're going to be detectives, we'll get a lot of use out of them."

The boys started toward the house, passing the old-fashioned barn on the property. Its first floor had been converted into a gymnasium which was used after school and on week ends by Frank and Joe and their friends.

The Hardy home, on the corner of High and Elm streets, was an old stone house set in a large, tree-shaded lawn. Right now, crocuses and miniature narcissi were sticking their heads through the light-green grass.

"Hello, Mother!" said Frank, as he pushed open the kitchen door.

Mrs. Hardy, a petite, pretty woman, looked up from the table on which she was stuffing a large roasting chicken and smiled.

Her sons kissed her affectionately and Joe asked, "Dad upstairs?"

"Yes, dear. He's in his study."

The study was Fenton Hardy's workshop. Adjoining it was a fine library which contained not only books but files of disguises, records of criminal cases, and translations of thousands of codes.

Walking into the study, Frank and Joe greeted their father. "We're reporting errand accomplished," Frank announced.

"Fine!" Mr. Hardy replied. Then he gave his sons a searching glance. "I'd say your trip netted you more than just my errand."

Frank and Joe had learned early in their boyhood that it was impossible to keep any secrets from their astute father. They assumed that this ability was one reason why he had been such a successful detective on the New York City police force before setting up a private practice in Bayport.

"We ran into some real excitement," Frank said, and told his father the whole story of Chet's missing jalopy, the wrecked car which they suspected had been a stolen one also, and the attempted holdup at the ferryboat office.

"Chet's counting on us to find his car," Joe added.

Frank grinned. "That is, unless the police find it first."

Mr. Hardy was silent for several seconds. Then he said, "Do you want a little advice? You know I never give it unless I'm asked for it." He chuckled.

"We'll need a lot of help," Joe answered.

Mr. Hardy said that to him the most interesting angle to the case was the fact that the suspect apparently used one or more wigs as a disguise. "He may have bought at least one of them in Bayport. I suggest that you boys make the rounds of all shops selling wigs and see what you can find out."

The boys glanced at the clock on their father's large desk, then Frank said, "We'll have time to do a little sleuthing before closing time. Let's go!"

The two boys made a dash for the door, then both stopped short. They did not have the slightest idea where they were going! Sheepishly Joe asked, "Dad, do you know which stores sell wigs?"

With a twinkle in his eyes, Mr. Hardy arose from the desk, walked into the library, and opened a file drawer labeled "W through Z." A moment later he pulled out a thick folder marked WIGS:

Manufacturers, distributors, and retail shops of the world.

"Why, Dad, I didn't know you had all this information—" Joe began.

His father merely smiled. He thumbed through the heavy sheaf of papers, and pulled one out.

"Bayport," he read. "Well, three of these places can be eliminated at once. They sell only women's hair pieces. Now let's see. Frank, get a paper and pencil. First there's Schwartz's Masquerade and Costume Shop. It's at 79 Renshaw Avenue. Then there's Flint's at Market and Pine, and one more: Ruben Brothers. That's on Main Street just this side of the railroad."

"Schwartz's is closest," Frank spoke up. "Let's try him first, Joe."

Hopefully the boys dashed out to their motor-cycles and hurried downtown. As they entered Schwartz's shop, a short, plump, smiling man came toward them.

"Well, you just got under the wire, fellows," he said, looking up at a large old-fashioned clock on the wall. "I was going to close up promptly tonight because a big shipment came in today and I never have time except after business hours to unpack and list my merchandise."

"Our errand won't take long," said Frank. "We're sons of Fenton Hardy, the detective. We'd like to know whether or not you recently sold a red wig to a man."

Mr. Schwartz shook his head. "I haven't sold a red wig in months, or even rented one. Everybody seems to want blond or brown or black lately. But you understand, I don't usually sell wigs at all. I rent 'em."

"I understand," said Frank. "We're just trying to find out about a man who uses a red wig as a disguise. We thought he might have bought or rented it here and that you would know his name."

Mr. Schwartz leaned across the counter. "This man you speak of—he sounds like a character. It's just possible he may come in to get a wig from me. If he does, I'll be glad to let you know."

The boys thanked the shopkeeper and were about to leave when Mr. Schwartz called, "Hold on a minute!"

The Hardys hoped that the dealer had suddenly remembered something important. This was not the case, however. With a grin the man asked the boys if they would like to help him open some cartons which had arrived and to try on the costumes.

"Those folks at the factory don't always get the sizes marked right," he said. "Would you be able to stay a few minutes and help me? I'll be glad to pay you."

"Oh, we don't want any money," Joe spoke up. "To tell you the truth, I'd like to see your costumes."

Mr. Schwartz locked the front door of his shop,

then led the boys into a rear room. It was so filled with costumes of all kinds and paraphernalia for theatrical work, plus piles of cartons, that Frank and Joe wondered how the man could ever find anything.

"Here is today's shipment," Mr. Schwartz said, pointing to six cartons standing not far from the rear entrance to his shop.

Together he and the boys slit open the boxes and one by one lifted out a king's robe, a queen's tiara, and a Little Bopeep costume. Suddenly Mr. Schwartz said:

"Here's a skeleton marked size thirty-eight. Would one of you boys mind trying it on?"

Frank picked up the costume, unzipped the back, and stepped into the skeleton outfit. It was tremendous on him and the ribs sagged ludicrously.

"Guess a fat man modeled for this," he remarked, holding the garment out to its full width.

At that moment there was a loud rap on the front door of the store. Mr. Schwartz made no move to answer it. "I'm closed," he said. "Let him rap."

Suddenly Frank had an idea. The thief who used wigs might be the late customer, coming on purpose at this hour to avoid meeting other people. Without a word to the others, he dashed through the doorway into the store and toward the front entrance.

He could vaguely see someone waiting to be admitted. But the stranger gave one look at the leaping, out-of-shape skeleton and disappeared in a flash. At the same moment Frank tripped and fell headlong.

Mr. Schwartz and Joe, hearing the crash, rushed out to see what had happened. Frank, hopelessly tangled in the skeleton attire, was helped to his feet. When he told the others why he had made his unsuccessful dash to the front door, they conceded he might have a point.

"But you sure scared him away in that outfit," Joe said, laughing. "He won't be back!"

The boys stayed for over half an hour helping Mr. Schwartz, then said good-by and went home.

"Monday we'll tackle those other two wig shops," said Frank.

The following morning the Hardy family attended church, then after dinner Frank and Joe told their parents they were going to ride out to see Chet Morton. "We've been invited to stay to supper," Frank added. "But we promise not to get home late."

The Hardys picked up Callie Shaw, who also had been invited. Gaily she perched on the seat behind Frank.

"Hold on, Callie," Joe teased. "Frank's a wild cyclist!"

The young people were greeted at the door of the Morton farmhouse by Chet's younger sister

Iola, dark-haired and pretty. Joe Hardy thought she was quite the nicest girl in Bayport High and dated her regularly.

As dusk came on, the five young people gathered in the Mortons' kitchen to prepare supper. Chet, who loved to eat, was in charge, and doled out various jobs to the others. When he finished, Joe remarked, "And what are you going to do, big boy?"

The stout youth grinned. "I'm the official taster."

A howl went up from the others. "No workee, no eatee," said Iola flatly.

Chet grinned. "Oh, well, if you insist, I'll make a little side dish for all of us. How about Welsh rabbit?"

"You're elected!" the others chorused, and Chet set to work.

The farmhouse kitchen was large and contained a group of windows in one corner. Here stood a large table, where the young people decided to eat. They had just sat down when the telephone rang. Chet got up and walked out in the hall to answer it. Within a minute he re-entered the kitchen, his eyes bulging.

"What's the matter?" Iola asked quickly.

"I— I've been th-threatened!" Chet replied.

"Threatened!" the others cried out. "How?"

Chet was so frightened he could hardly speak, but he managed to make the others understand that a man had just said on the telephone, "You'll never get your jalopy back. And if you don't lay off trying to find me or your car, you're going to get hurt!"

"Whew!" cried Joe. "This is getting serious!"

Callie and Iola had clutched their throats and were staring wild-eyed at Chet. Frank, about to speak, happened to glance out the window toward the barn. For an instant he thought his eyes were playing tricks on him. But no! They were not. A figure was sneaking from the barn and down the lane toward the highway.

"Fellows!" he cried suddenly. "Follow me!"

CHAPTER IV

Red Versus Yellow

By the time the Hardy boys and Chet had raced from the Mortons' kitchen, the prowler was not in sight. Thinking he had run across one of the fields, the three pursuers scattered in various directions to search. Joe struck out straight ahead and pressed his ear to the ground to listen for receding footsteps. He could hear none. Presently the three boys met once more to discuss their failure to catch up to the man, and to question why he had been there.

"Do you think he was a thief?" Joe asked Chet. "What would he steal?"

"Search me," the stout boy replied. "Let's take a look."

"I believe he was carrying something, but I couldn't see what it was," Frank revealed.

The barn door had not been closed yet for the night and the boys walked in. Chet turned on the lights and the searchers gazed around.

"Look!" Frank cried suddenly.

He pointed to the floor below the telephone extension in the barn. There lay a man's gray wig.

"The intruder's!" Joe exclaimed.

"It sure looks so," Frank agreed. "And something must have scared him. In his hurry to get away he must have dropped this."

Frank picked up the wig and examined it carefully for a clue. "No identifying mark in it. Say, I have an idea," he burst out. "That man phoned you from here, Chet."

"You mean he's the one who threatened me?"

"Yes. If you know how, you can call your own telephone number from an extension."

"That's right."

Chet was wagging his head. "You mean that guy bothered to come all the way here to use this phone to threaten me? Why?"

Both Hardys said they felt the man had not come specifically for that reason. There was another more important one. "We must figure it out. Chet, you ought to be able to answer that better than anybody else. What is there, or was there, in this barn to interest such a person?"

The stout boy scratched his head and let his eyes wander around the building. "It wouldn't be any of the livestock," he said slowly. "And it couldn't be hay or feed." Suddenly Chet snapped his fingers. "Maybe I have the answer. Wait a minute, fellows."

On the floor lay a man's wig

He disappeared from the barn and made a bee-line for the garage. Chet hurried inside but was back in a few seconds.

"I have it!" he shouted. "That guy came here to get the spare tire for the jalopy."

"The one you had is gone?" Frank asked.

Chet nodded. He suggested that perhaps the man was not too far away. He might be on some side road changing the tire. "Let's find out," he urged.

Although the Hardys felt that it would be a use-less search, they agreed to go along. They got on their motorcycles, with Chet riding behind Joe. The boys went up one road and down another, covering the territory very thoroughly. They saw no parked car.

"Not even any evidence that a driver pulled off the road and stayed to change a tire," Frank re-marked. "No footprints, no tool marks, no treads."

"That guy must have had somebody around to pick him up," Chet concluded with a sigh.

"Cheer up, Chet," Frank said, as they walked back to the house. "That spare tire may turn out to be a clue in this case."

When the boys entered the kitchen again, they were met with anxious inquiries from Callie and Iola.

"What in the world were you doing—dashing

out of here without a word?" Callie asked in a shaking voice.

"Yes, what's going on? You had us frightened silly," Iola joined in. "First Chet gets a threatening phone call, and then suddenly all three of you run out of the house like madmen!"

"Calm down, girls," Frank said soothingly. "I saw a prowler, and we were looking for him, but all we found was this!" He tossed the gray wig onto a chair in the hall.

Suddenly there was a loud wail from Chet. "My Welsh rabbit! It's been standing so long it will be ruined!"

Iola began to giggle. "Oh, you men!" she said. "Do you suppose Callie and I would let all that good cheese go to waste? We kept that Welsh rabbit at just the right temperature and it isn't spoiled at all."

Chet looked relieved, as he and the others took their places at the table. Although there was a great deal of bantering during the meal, the conversation in the main revolved around Chet's missing jalopy and the thief who evidently wore hair disguises to suit his fancy.

Frank and Joe asked Chet if they might take along the gray wig and examine it more thoroughly. There might be some kind of mark on it to indicate either the maker or the owner. Chet readily agreed.

But when supper was over, Callie said to Frank with a teasing gleam in her eyes, "Why don't you hot-shot sleuths examine that wig now? I'd like to watch your super-duper methods."

"Just for that, I will," said Frank.

He went to get the wig from the hall chair, and then laid it on the kitchen table. From his pocket he took a small magnifying glass and carefully examined every inch of the lining of the wig.

"Nothing here," he said presently.

The hair was thoroughly examined and parted strand by strand to see if there were any identifying designations on the hair piece. Frank could discover nothing.

"I'm afraid this isn't going to help us much," he said in disgust. "But I'll show it to the different wig men in town."

As he finished speaking the telephone rang and Iola went to answer it. Chet turned white and looked nervous. Was the caller the man who had threatened him? And what did he want?

Presently Iola returned to the kitchen, a worried frown on her face. "It's a man for you, Chet. He wouldn't give his name."

Trembling visibly, Chet walked slowly to the telephone. The others followed and listened.

"Ye-yes, I'm Chet Morton. N-no, I haven't got my car back."

There was a long silence, as the person on the other end of the line spoke rapidly.

"B-but I haven't any money," Chet said finally. "I— Well, okay, I'll let you know."

Chet hung up and wobbled to a nearby chair. The others bombarded him with questions.

The stout boy took a deep breath, then said, "I can get my jalopy back. But the man wants a lot of money for the information as to where it is."

"Oh, I'm glad you're going to get your car back!" Callie exclaimed.

"But I haven't got any money," Chet groaned.

"Who's the man?" Frank demanded.

There was another long pause before Chet answered. Then, looking at the waiting group before him, he announced simply, "Smuff. Oscar Smuff!"

His listeners gasped in astonishment. This was the last thing they expected to hear. The detective was selling information as to where Chet would find his missing jalopy!

"Why, that cheap so-and-so!" Joe cried out angrily.

Chet explained that Smuff had said he was not in business for his health. He had to make a living and any information which he dug up as a detective should be properly paid for.

Frank shrugged. "I suppose Smuff has a point there. How much does he want for the information, Chet?"

"His fee is twenty-five dollars!"

"What!" the others cried out.

After a long consultation it was decided that

the young people would pool their resources. Whatever sum they could collect toward the twenty-five dollars would be offered to Oscar Smuff to lead them to Chet's car.

"But make it very plain," Frank admonished, "that if it's not your jalopy Smuff leads us to, you won't pay him one nickel."

Chet put in a call to Smuff's home. As expected, the detective grumbled at the offer of ten dollars but finally accepted it. He said he would pick up the boys in half an hour and take them to the spot.

About this time Mr. and Mrs. Morton returned home. Chet and Iola's father was a good-looking, jolly man with his son's same general build and coloring. He was in the real-estate business in Bayport and ran the farm as a hobby.

Mrs. Morton was an older edition of her daughter Iola and just as witty and lighthearted. But when she learned what had transpired and that her son had been threatened, she was worried.

"You boys must be very careful," Mrs. Morton advised. "From what I hear about Smuff, this red-haired thief could easily put one over on him. So watch your step!"

Chet promised that they would.

"Good luck!" Callie called out, as Smuff beeped his horn outside the door. "And don't be too late. I want to hear the news before I have to go home."

Frank, Joe, and Chet found Smuff entirely un-communicative about where they were going. He seemed to enjoy the role he was playing.

"I knew I'd be the one to break this case," he boasted.

Joe could not resist the temptation of asking Smuff if he was going to lead them to the thief as well as to the car. The detective flushed in embarrassment and admitted that he did not have full details yet on this part of the mystery.

"But it won't be long before I capture that fellow," he assured the boys. They managed to keep their faces straight and only hoped that they were not now on a wild-goose chase.

Twenty minutes later Smuff pulled into the town of Ducksworth and drove straight to a used-car lot. Stopping, he announced, "Well, here we are. Get ready to fork over that money, Chet."

Smuff nodded to the attendant in charge, then led the boys down a long aisle past row after row of cars to where several jalopies were lined up against a rear fence. Turning left, the detective finally paused before a bright red car.

"Here you are!" said Smuff grandly, extending his right hand toward Chet. "My money, please."

The stout boy as well as the Hardys stared at the jalopy. There was no question but that it was the same make and model as Chet's.

"The thief thought he could disguise it by painting it red," Smuff explained.

"Is that your guess?" Frank asked quietly.

Oscar Smuff frowned. "How else could you figure it?" he asked.

"Then there'll be yellow paint under the red," Frank went on. "Let's take a look to make sure."

It was evident that Smuff did not like this procedure. "So you doubt me, eh?" he asked in an unpleasant tone.

"Anybody can get fooled," Frank told him. "Well, Chet, let's operate on this car."

The detective stood by sullenly as Frank pulled out a penknife and began to scrape the red paint off part of the fender.

CHAPTER V

The Hunt Is Intensified

"HEY!" Oscar Smuff shouted. "You be careful with that penknife! The man who owns this place don't want you ruinin' his cars!"

Frank Hardy looked up at the detective. "I've watched my father scrape off flecks of paint many times. The way he does it, you wouldn't know anybody had made a mark."

Smuff grunted. "But you're not your father. Easy there!"

As cautiously as possible Frank picked off flecks of the red paint in a spot where it would hardly be noticeable. Taking a flashlight from his pocket, he trained it on the spot.

Joe, leaning over his brother's shoulder, said, "There was light-blue paint under this red, not yellow."

"Right," Frank agreed, eying Smuff intently.

The detective reddened. "You fellows trying to

tell me this isn't Chet's jalopy?" he demanded. "Well, I'm telling you it is, and I'm right!"

"Oh, we haven't said you're wrong," Joe spoke up quickly. Secretly he was hoping that this was Chet's car, but reason told him it was not.

"We'll try another place," Frank said, straightening up, and walking around to a fender on the opposite side.

Here, too, the test indicated that the car had been painted light blue before the red coat had been put over it.

"Well, maybe the thief put blue on and then red," said Smuff stubbornly.

Frank grinned. "We'll go a little deeper. If the owner of this establishment objects, we'll pay for having the fenders painted."

But though Frank went down through several layers of paint, he could not find any sign of yellow.

All this time Chet had been walking round and round the car, looking intently at it inside and out. Even before Frank announced that he was sure this was not the missing jalopy, Chet was convinced of it himself.

"The Queen had a long, thin dent in the right rear fender," he said. "And that seat cushion by the door had a little split in it. I don't think the thief would have bothered to fix them up."

Chet showed his keen disappointment, but he was glad that the Hardys had come along to help him prove the truth. But Smuff was not giving up the money so easily.

"You haven't proved a thing," he said. "The man who runs this place admitted that maybe this is a stolen car. The fellow who sold it to him said he lived on a farm outside Bayport."

The Hardys and Chet were taken aback for a moment by this information. But in a moment Frank said, "Let's go talk to the owner. We'll find out more about the person who brought this car in."

The man who ran the used-car lot was very co-operative. He readily answered all questions the Hardys put to him. The bill of sale revealed that the former owner of the red jalopy was Melvin Schuster of Bayport.

"Why, we know him!" Frank spoke up. "He goes to Bayport High—at least, he did. He and his family moved far away. That's probably why he sold his car."

"But Mr. Smuff said you suspected the car was stolen," Joe put in.

The used-car lot owner smiled. "I'm afraid maybe Mr. Smuff put that idea in my head. I did say that the person seemed in an awful hurry to get rid of the car and sold it very cheap. Sometimes when that happens, we dealers are a little afraid to take the responsibility of buying a car, in case it is stolen property. But at the time Mr. Schuster came in, I thought everything was on the level and bought his jalopy."

Frank said that he was sure everything was all right, and after the dealer described Melvin Schuster, there was no question but that he was the owner.

Smuff was completely crestfallen. Without a word he started for his own car and the boys followed. The detective did not talk on the way back to the Morton farm, and the boys, feeling rather sorry for him, spoke of matters other than the car incident.

As the Hardys and Chet walked into the Morton home, the two girls rushed forward. "Did you find it?" Iola asked eagerly.

Chet sighed. "Another one of Smuff's bluffs," he said disgustedly. He handed back the money which his friends had given to help pay the detective.

Frank and Joe said good-by, went for their motorcycles, and took Callie home. Then they returned to their own house, showered, and went to bed.

As soon as school was over the next day, they took the gray wig and visited Schwartz's shop. The owner assured them that the hair piece had not come from his store.

"It's a very cheap one," the man said rather disdainfully.

Frank and Joe visited Flint's and Ruben Brothers' shops as well. Neither place had sold the gray wig. Furthermore, neither of them had had a customer in many weeks who had wanted a red wig, or who was in the habit of using wigs or toupees of various colors.

"Today's sleuthing was a complete washout," Joe reported that night to his father.

The famous detective smiled. "Don't be discouraged," he said. "I can tell you that one bit of success makes up for a hundred false trails."

As the boys were undressing for bed later, Frank reminded his brother that the following day was a school holiday. "That'll give us hours and hours to work on the case," he said enthusiastically.

"What do you suggest we do?" Joe asked.

Frank shrugged. Several ideas were brought up by the brothers, but one which Joe proposed was given preference. They would get hold of a large group of their friends. On the theory that the thief could not have driven a long distance away because of the police alarm, the boys would make an extensive search in the surrounding area for Chet's jalopy.

"We'll hunt in every possible hiding place," he stated.

Early the next morning Frank hurried to the telephone and put in one call after another to "the gang." These included, besides Chet Morton, Allen Hooper, nicknamed Biff because of his fondness for a distant relative who was a boxer named Biff; Jerry Gilroy, Phil Cohen, and Tony Prito. All were students at Bayport High and prominent in various sports.

The five boys were eager to co-operate. They agreed to assemble at the Hardy home at nine o'clock. In the meantime, Frank and Joe would lay out a plan of action.

As soon as breakfast was over the Hardys told their father what they had in mind and asked if he had any suggestions on how they might go about their search.

"Take a map," he said, "with our house as a radius and cut pie-shaped sections. I suggest that two boys work together."

By nine o'clock his sons had mapped out the search in detail. The first recruit to arrive was Tony Prito, a lively boy with a good sense of humor. He was followed in a moment by Phil Cohen, a quiet, intelligent boy.

"Put us to work," said Tony. "I brought one of my father's trucks that he isn't going to use to-day." Tony's father was in the contracting business. "I can cover a lot of miles in it."

Frank suggested that Tony and Phil work together. He showed them the map, with Bayport as the center of a great circle, cut into four equal sections.

"Suppose you take from nine o'clock to twelve on this dial we've marked. Mother has agreed to stay at home all day and act as clearing house for our reports. Call in every hour."

"Will do," Tony promised. "Come on, Phil. Let's get going!"

The two boys were just starting off when Biff and Jerry arrived at the Hardy home on motorcycles. Biff, blond and long-legged, had an ambling gait, with which he could cover a tremendous amount of territory in a short time. Jerry, an excellent fielder on Bayport High's baseball team, was of medium height, wiry, and strong.

Biff and Jerry were assigned to the section on the map designated six to nine o'clock. They were given further instructions on sleuthing, then started off on their quest.

"Where's Chet?" Mr. Hardy asked his sons. "Wasn't he going to help in the search?"

"He probably overslept. Chet's been known to do that," Frank said with a grin.

"He also might have taken time for a double breakfast," Joe suggested.

Mrs. Hardy, who had stepped to the front porch, called, "Here he comes now. Isn't that Mr. Morton's car?"

"Yes, it is," Frank replied.

Chet's father let him off in front of the Hardy home and the stout boy hurried to the porch. "Good morning, Mrs. Hardy. Good morning, Mr. Hardy. Hi, chums!" he said cheerily. "Sorry to be late. My dad had a lot of phoning to do before he left. I was afraid if I'd tried to walk here, I wouldn't have arrived until tomorrow."

At this point Mr. Hardy spoke up. "As I said before, I think you boys should work in twos. There are only three of you to take care of half the territory." The detective suddenly grinned boyishly. "How about me teaming up with one of you?"

Frank and Joe looked at their dad in delight. "You mean it?" Frank cried out. "I'll choose you as my partner right now."

"I have a further suggestion," the detective said. "It's not going to take you fellows more than three hours to cover the area you've laid out. And there's an additional section I think you might look into."

"What's that?" Joe inquired.

"Willow Grove. That's a park area, but there's also a lot of tangled woodland to one side of it. Good place to hide a stolen car."

Mr. Hardy suggested that the boys meet for a picnic lunch at Willow Grove and later do some sleuthing in the vicinity. "That is, provided you haven't found Chet's jalopy by that time."

Mrs. Hardy spoke up. "I'll fix a nice lunch for all of you," she offered.

"That sure would be swell," Chet said hastily. "You make grand picnic lunches, Mrs. Hardy."

Frank and Joe liked the plan, and it was decided that the boys would have the picnic whether or not they had found the jalopy by one o'clock. Mrs. Hardy said she would relay the news to the other boys when they phoned in.

Chet and Joe set off on the Hardy boys' motorcycles, taking the twelve-to-three segment on the map. Then Mr. Hardy and Frank drove off for the three-to-six area.

Hour after hour went by, with the searchers constantly on the alert. Every garage, public and private, every little-used road, every patch of woods was thoroughly investigated. There was no sign of Chet's missing yellow jalopy. Finally at one o'clock Frank and his father returned to the Hardy home. A few moments later Joe and Chet returned and a huge picnic lunch was stowed aboard the two motorcycles.

When the three boys reached the picnic area they were required to park their motorcycles outside the fence. They unstrapped the lunch baskets and carried them down to the lake front. The other boys were already there.

"Too bad we can't go swimming," Tony remarked, "but this water's pretty cold."

Quickly they unpacked the food and assembled around one of the park picnic tables.

"Um! Yum! Chicken sandwiches!" Chet cried gleefully.

During the meal the boys exchanged reports on their morning's sleuthing. All had tried hard but failed to find any trace of the missing car.

"Our work hasn't ended," Frank reminded the others. "But I'm so stuffed I'm going to rest a while before I start out again."

All the other boys but Joe Hardy felt the same way and lay down on the grass for a nap. Joe, eager to find out whether or not the woods to their right held the secret of the missing car, plunged off alone through the underbrush.

He searched for twenty minutes without finding a clue to any automobile. He was on the point of returning and waiting for the other boys when he saw a small clearing ahead of him. It appeared to be part of an abandoned roadway.

Excitedly Joe pushed on through the dense undergrowth. It was in a low-lying part of the grove and the ground was wet. At one point it was quite muddy, and it was here that Joe saw something that aroused his curiosity.

"A tire! Then maybe an automobile has been in here," he muttered to himself, although there were no tire marks in the immediate vicinity. "No footprints, either. I guess someone tossed this tire here."

Remembering his father's admonitions on the value of developing one's powers of observation, Joe went closer and examined the tire.

"That tread," he thought excitedly, "looks familiar."

He gazed at it until he was sure, then dashed back to the other boys.

"I've found a clue!" he cried out. "Come on, everybody!"

CHAPTER VI

The Robbery

JOE HARDY quickly led the way into the swampy area as the other boys trooped along, everyone talking at once. When they reached the spot, Chet examined the tire and exclaimed:

"There's no mistake about it! This is one of the tires! When the thief put on the new one, he threw this away."

"Perhaps the Queen is still around," suggested Frank quickly. "The thief may have picked this road as a good place to hide your jalopy until he could make a getaway."

"It would be an ideal place," Chet agreed. "People coming to Willow Grove have to park at the gate, so nobody would come in here. But this old road comes in from the main highway. Let's take a look, fellows."

A scrutinizing search was begun along the abandoned road in the direction of the highway. A moment later Frank and Chet, in the lead, cried out simultaneously.

"Here's a bypath! And here are tire marks!" Frank exclaimed. To one side was a narrow roadway, almost overgrown with weeds and low bushes. It led from the abandoned road into the depths of the woods.

Without hesitation Frank and Chet plunged into it. Presently the roadway widened out, then wound about a heavy clump of trees. It came to an end in a wide clearing.

In the clearing stood Chet Morton's lost jalopy!

"My Queen!" he yelled in delight. "Her own license plates!"

His shout was heard by the rest of the boys, who came on a run. Chet's joy was boundless. He examined the car with minute care, while his chums crowded around. At last he straightened up with a smile of satisfaction.

"She hasn't been damaged a bit. All ready to run. The thief just hid the old bus in here and made a getaway. Come on, fellows, climb aboard. Free ride to the highway!"

Before leaving, the Hardys examined footprints left by the thief. "He wore sneakers," Frank observed.

Suddenly Chet swung open the door and looked on the floor. "You mean he wore *my* sneakers. They're gone."

"And carried his own shoes," Joe observed. "Very clever. Well, that washes out one clue. Can't trace the man by his shoe prints."

"Let's go!" Chet urged.

He jumped into the car and in a few seconds the engine roared. There was barely sufficient room in the clearing to permit him to turn the jalopy about. When he swung around and headed up the bypath, the boys gave a cheer and hastened to clamber aboard.

Lurching and swaying, the car reached the abandoned road and from there made the run to the main highway. The boys transferred to Tony's truck and the motorcycles, and formed a parade into Bayport, with Frank and Joe in the lead. It was their intention to ride up to police headquarters and announce their success to Chief Collig.

"And I hope Smuff will be around," Chet gloated.

As the grinning riders came down Main Street, however, they noticed that no one paid any attention to them, and there seemed to be an unusual air of mystery in the town. People were standing in little groups, gesticulating and talking earnestly.

Presently the Hardys saw Oscar Smuff striding along with a portentous frown. Joe called out to him. "What's going on, detective? You notice we found Chet's car."

"I've got something more important than stolen cars to worry— Hey, what's that?" Detective Smuff stared blankly, as the full import of the discovery filtered his consciousness.

The boys waited for Smuff's praise, but he did not give it. Instead, he said, "I got a big mystery to solve. The Tower Mansion has been robbed!"

"Good night!" the Hardys chorused.

Tower Mansion was one of the show places of Bayport. Few people in the city had ever been permitted to enter the place and the admiration which the palatial building excited was solely by reason of its exterior appearance. But the first thing a newcomer to Bayport usually asked was, "Who owns that house with the towers over on the hill?"

It was an immense, rambling stone structure overlooking the bay, and could be seen for miles, silhouetted against the sky line like an ancient feudal castle. The resemblance to a castle was heightened by the fact that from each of the far ends of the mansion arose a high tower.

One of these had been built when the mansion was erected by Major Applegate, an eccentric, retired old Army man who had made a fortune by lucky real-estate deals. Years ago there had been many parties and dances in the mansion.

But the Applegate family had become scattered until at last there remained in the old home only Hurd Applegate and his sister Adelia. They lived in the vast, lonely mansion at the present time.

Hurd Applegate was a man about sixty, tall, and stooped. His life seemed to be devoted now to the collection of rare stamps. But a few years before he had built a new tower on the mansion, a duplicate of the original one.

His sister Adelia was a maiden lady of uncertain years. Well-dressed women in Bayport were amused by her clothes. She dressed in clashing colors and unbecoming styles. Hurd and Adelia Applegate were reputed to be enormously wealthy, although they lived simply, kept only a few servants, and never had visitors.

"Tell us about the theft," Joe begged Smuff.

But the detective waved his hand airily. "You'll have to find out yourselves," he retorted as he hurried off.

Frank and Joe called good-by to their friends and headed for home. As they arrived, the boys saw Hurd Applegate just leaving the house. The man tapped the steps with his cane as he came down them. When he heard the boys' motorcycles he gave them a piercing glance.

"Good day!" he growled in a grudging manner and went on his way.

"He must have been asking Dad to take the case," Frank said to his brother, as they pulled into the garage.

The boys rushed into the house, eager to find out more about the robbery. In the front hallway they met their father.

"We heard the Tower Mansion has been robbed," said Joe.

Mr. Hardy nodded. "Yes. Mr. Applegate was just here to tell me about it. He wants me to handle the case."

"How much was taken?"

Mr. Hardy smiled. "Well, I don't suppose it will do any harm to tell you. The safe in the Applegate library was opened. The loss will be about forty thousand dollars, all in securities and jewels."

"Whew!" exclaimed Frank. "What a haul! When did it happen?"

"Either last night or this morning. Mr. Applegate did not get up until after ten o'clock this morning and did not go into the library until nearly noon. It was then that he discovered the theft."

"How was the safe opened?"

"By using the combination. It was opened either by someone who knew the set of numbers or else by a very clever thief who could detect the noise of the tumblers. I'm going up to the house in a few minutes. Mr. Applegate is to call for me."

"I'd like to go along," Joe said eagerly.

"So would I," Frank declared.

Mr. Hardy looked at his sons and smiled. "Well, if you want to be detectives, I suppose it is about as good a chance as any to watch a crime investigation from the inside. If Mr. Applegate doesn't object, you may come with me."

A few minutes later a foreign-make, chauffeur-driven car drew up before the Hardy home. Mr.

Applegate was seated in the rear, his chin resting on his cane. The three Hardys went outside. When the detective mentioned the boys' request, the man merely grunted assent and moved over. Frank and Joe stepped in after their father. The car headed toward Tower Mansion.

"I don't really need a detective in this case!" Hurd Applegate snapped. "Don't need one at all. It's as clear as the nose on your face. I *know* who took the stuff. But I can't prove it."

"Whom do you suspect?" Fenton Hardy asked.

"Only one man in the world could have taken the jewels and securities. Robinson!"

"Robinson?"

"Yes. Henry Robinson—the caretaker. He's the man."

The Hardy boys looked at each other in consternation. Henry Robinson, the caretaker of the Tower Mansion, was the father of one of their closest chums! Perry Robinson, nicknamed "Slim," was the son of the accused man!

That his father should be blamed for the robbery seemed absurd to the Hardy boys. They had met Mr. Robinson upon several occasions and he had appeared to be a good-natured, easygoing man with high principles.

"I don't believe he's guilty," Frank whispered.

"Neither do I," returned his brother.

"What makes you suspect Robinson?" Mr. Hardy asked Hurd Applegate.

"He's the only person besides my sister and me who ever saw that safe opened and closed. He could have learned the combination if he'd kept his eyes and ears open, which I'm sure he did."

"Is that your only reason for suspecting him?"

"No. This morning he paid off a nine-hundred-dollar note at the bank. And I know for a fact he didn't have more than one hundred dollars to his name a few days ago. Now where did he raise nine hundred dollars so suddenly?"

"Perhaps he has a good explanation," Mr. Hardy suggested.

"Oh, he'll have an explanation all right!" sniffed Mr. Applegate. "But it will have to be a mighty good one to satisfy me."

The automobile was now speeding up the wide driveway that led to Tower Mansion and within a few minutes stopped at the front entrance. Mr. Hardy and the two boys accompanied the eccentric man into the house.

"Nothing has been disturbed in the library since the discovery of the theft," he said, leading the way there.

Mr. Hardy examined the open safe, then took a special magnifying glass from his pocket. With minute care he inspected the dial of the combination lock. Next he walked to each window and the door to examine them for fingerprints. He asked Mr. Applegate to hold his fingers up to a strong light and got a clear view of the whorls and lines on the inside of the tips. At last he shook his head.

"A smooth job," he observed. "The thief must have worn gloves. All the fingerprints in the room, Mr. Applegate, seem to be yours."

"No use looking for fingerprints or any other evidence!" Mr. Applegate barked impatiently. "It was Robinson, I tell you."

"Perhaps it would be a good idea for me to ask him a few questions," Mr. Hardy advised.

Mr. Applegate rang for one of the servants and instructed him to tell the caretaker to come to the library at once. Mr. Hardy glanced at the boys and suggested they wait in the hallway.

"It might prove less embarrassing to Mr. Robinson that way," he said in a low voice.

Frank and Joe readily withdrew. In the hall they met Mr. Robinson and his son Perry. The man was calm, but pale, and at the doorway he patted Slim on the shoulder.

"Don't worry," he said. "Everything will be all right." With that he entered the library.

Slim turned to his two friends. "It's got to be!" he cried out. "My dad is innocent!"

CHAPTER VII

The Arrest

FRANK and Joe were determined to help their chum prove his father's innocence. They shared his conviction that Mr. Robinson was not guilty.

"Of course he's innocent," Frank agreed. "He'll be able to clear himself all right, Slim."

"But things look pretty black right now," the boy said. He was white-faced and shaken. "Unless Mr. Hardy can catch the real thief, I'm afraid Dad will be blamed for the robbery."

"Everybody knows your father is honest," said Joe consolingly. "He has been a faithful employee —even Mr. Applegate will have to admit that."

"Which won't help him much if he can't clear himself of the charge. And Dad admits that he did know the combination of the safe, although of course he'd never use it."

"He knew it?" repeated Joe, surprised.

"Dad learned the combination accidentally. It was so simple one couldn't forget it. This was how it happened. One day when he was cleaning the library fireplace, he found a piece of paper with numbers on it. He studied them and decided they were the safe combination. Dad laid the paper on the desk. The window was open and he figured the breeze must have blown the paper to the floor."

"Does Mr. Applegate know that?"

"Not yet. But Dad is going to tell him now. He realizes it will look bad for him, but he's going to give Mr. Applegate the truth."

From the library came the hum of voices. The harsh tones of Hurd Applegate occasionally rose above the murmur of conversation and finally the boys heard Mr. Robinson's voice rise sharply.

"I *didn't* do it! I tell you I *didn't* take that money!"

"Then where did you get the nine hundred you paid on that note?" demanded Mr. Applegate.

Silence.

"Where did you get it?"

"I'm not at liberty to tell you or anyone else."

"Why not?"

"I got the money honestly—that's all I can say about it."

"Oh, ho!" exclaimed Mr. Applegate. "You got the money honestly, yet you can't tell me where it came from! A pretty story! If you got the money honestly you shouldn't be ashamed to tell where it came from."

"I'm not ashamed. I can only say again, I'm not at liberty to talk about it."

"Mighty funny thing that you should get nine hundred dollars so quickly. You were pretty hard up last week, weren't you? Had to ask for an advance on your month's wages."

"That is true."

"And then the day of this robbery you suddenly have nine hundred dollars that you can't explain."

Mr. Hardy's calm voice broke in. "Of course I don't like to pry into your private affairs, Mr. Robinson," he said, "but it would be best if you would clear up this matter of the money."

"I know it looks bad," replied the caretaker doggedly. "But I've made a promise I can't break."

"And you admit being familiar with the combination of the safe, too!" broke in Mr. Applegate. "I didn't know that before. Why didn't you tell me?"

"I didn't consider it important."

"And yet you come and tell me now!"

"I have nothing to conceal. If I had taken the securities and jewels I wouldn't be telling you that I knew the combination."

"Yes," agreed Mr. Hardy, "that's a point in your favor, Mr. Robinson."

"Is it?" asked Mr. Applegate. "Robinson's just clever enough to think up a trick like that. He'd figure that by appearing to be honest, I'd believe he is honest and couldn't have committed this robbery. Very clever. But not clever enough. There's plenty of evidence right this minute to convict him, and I'm not going to delay any further."

In a moment Mr. Applegate's voice continued, "Police station? Hello . . . Police station? . . . This is Applegate speaking—Applegate—Hurd Applegate. . . . Well, we've found our man in that robbery. . . . Yes, Robinson. . . . You thought so, eh?—So did I, but I wasn't sure. . . . He has practically convicted himself by his own story. . . . Yes, I want him arrested. . . . You'll be up right away? . . . Fine. . . . Good-by."

"You're not going to have me arrested, Mr. Applegate?" the caretaker cried out in alarm.

"Why not? You're the thief!"

"It might have been better to wait a while," Mr. Hardy interposed. "At least until there was more evidence."

"What more evidence do we want, Mr. Hardy," the owner of Tower Mansion sneered. "If Robinson wants to return the jewels and securities I'll have the charge withdrawn—but that's all."

"I can't return them! I didn't take them!" Mr. Robinson defended himself.

"You'll have plenty of time to think," Mr. Applegate declared. "You'll be in the penitentiary a long time—a long time."

In the hallway the boys listened in growing excitement and dismay. The case had taken an abrupt and tragic turn. Slim looked as though he might collapse under the strain.

"My dad's innocent," the boy muttered over and over again, clenching his fists. "I *know* he is. They can't arrest him. He never stole anything in his life!"

Frank patted his friend on the shoulder. "Brace up, pal," he advised. "It looks discouraging just now, but I'm sure your father will be able to clear himself."

"I— I'll have to tell Mother," stammered Slim. "This will break her heart. And my sisters—"

Frank and Joe followed the boy down the hallway and along a corridor that led to the east wing of the mansion. There, in a neat but sparsely furnished apartment, they found Mrs. Robinson, a gentle, kind-faced woman, who was lame. She was seated in a chair by the window, anxiously waiting. Her two daughters, Paula and Tessie, twelve-year-old twins, were at her side, and all looked up in expectation as the boys came in.

"What news, son?" Mrs. Robinson asked bravely, after she had greeted the Hardys.

"Bad, Mother."

"They're not—they're not—arresting him?" cried Paula, springing forward.

Perry nodded wordlessly.

"But they can't!" Tessie protested. "Dad *couldn't* do anything like that! It's wrong—"

Frank, looking at Mrs. Robinson, saw her suddenly slump over in a faint. He sprang forward and caught the woman in his arms as she was about to fall to the floor.

"Mother!" cried Slim in terror, as Frank laid Mrs. Robinson on a couch, then he said quickly to his sister, "Paula, bring the smelling salts and her special medicine."

Perry explained that at times undue excitement caused an "attack." "I shouldn't have told her about Dad," the boy chided himself.

"She'd have to know it sooner or later," Joe said kindly.

In a moment Paula returned with the bottle of smelling salts and medicine. The inhalant brought her mother back to consciousness, and Paula then gave Mrs. Robinson the medicine. In a few moments the woman completely revived and apologized for having worried everyone.

"I admit it was a dreadful shock to think my husband has been arrested," she said, "but surely something can be done to prove his innocence."

Instantly Frank and Joe assured her they would do everything they could to find the real thief, because they too felt that Mr. Robinson was not guilty.

The next morning, as the brothers were dressing in their room at home, Frank remarked, "There's a great deal about this case that hasn't come to the surface yet. It's just possible that the man who stole Chet Morton's car may have had something to do with the theft."

Joe agreed. "He was a criminal—that much is certain. He stole an automobile and he tried to hold up the ticket office, so why not another robbery?"

"Right, Joe. I just realized that we never inspected Chet's car for any clues to the thief, so let's do it."

The stout boy did not bring his jalopy to school that day, so the Hardys had to submerge their curiosity until classes and baseball practice were over. Then, when Mrs. Morton picked up Chet and Iola, Frank and Joe went home with them.

"I'll look under the seats," Joe offered.

"And I'll search the trunk compartment." Frank walked to the back of the car and raised the cover. He began rooting under rags, papers, and discarded schoolbooks. Presently he gave a cry of victory.

"Here it is! The best evidence in the world!"

Joe and Chet rushed to his side as he held up a man's red wig.

Frank said excitedly, "Maybe there's a clue in this hair piece!"

An examination failed to reveal any, but Frank said he would like to show the wig to his father. He covered it with a handkerchief and put it carefully in an inner pocket. Chet drove the Hardys home.

They assumed that their father was in his study on the second floor, and rushed up there and into the room without ceremony.

"Dad, we've found a clue!" Joe cried. Then he stepped back, embarrassed, as he realized there was someone else in the room.

"Sorry!" said Frank. The boys would have retreated, but Mr. Hardy's visitor turned around and they saw that he was Perry Robinson.

"It's only me," said Slim. "Don't go."

"Hi, Slim!"

"Perry has been trying to shed a little more light on the Tower robbery," explained Mr. Hardy. "But what is this clue you're talking about?"

"It might concern the robbery," replied Frank. "It's about the red-haired man." He took the wig from his pocket and told where he had found it.

Mr. Hardy's interest was kindled at once. "This seems to link up a pretty good chain of evidence. The man who passed you on the shore road wrecked the car he was driving, then stole Chet's, and afterward tried to hold up the ticket office. When he failed there, he tried another and more successful robbery at the Tower."

"Do you really think the wig might help us solve the Tower robbery?" asked Perry, taking hope.

"Possibly."

"I was just telling your father," Slim went on, "that I saw a strange man lurking around the grounds of the mansion two days before the robbery. I didn't think anything of it at the time, and in the shock of Dad's arrest I forgot about it."

"Did you get a good look at him? Could you describe him?" Frank asked.

"I'm afraid I can't. It was in the evening. I was sitting by a window, studying, and happened to look up. I saw this fellow moving about among the trees. Later, I heard one of the dogs barking in another part of the grounds. Shortly afterward, I saw someone running across the lawn. I thought he was just a tramp."

"Did he wear a hat or a cap?"

"As near as I can remember, it was a cap. His clothes were dark."

"And you couldn't see his face?"

"No."

"Well, it's not much to go on," said Mr. Hardy, "but it might be linked up with Frank and Joe's idea that the man who stole the jalopy may still have been hanging around Bayport." The detective thought deeply for a few moments. "I'll bring all these facts to Mr. Applegate's attention, and I'm also going to have a talk with the police authorities. I feel they haven't enough evidence to warrant holding your father, Perry."

"Do you think you can have him released?" the boy asked eagerly.

"I'm sure of it. In fact, I believe Mr. Applegate

is beginning to realize now that he made a mistake."

"It will be wonderful if we can have Dad back with us again," said Perry. "Of course things won't be the same for him. He'll be under a cloud of suspicion as long as this mystery isn't cleared up. I suppose Mr. Applegate won't employ him or anyone else."

"All the more reason why we should get busy and clear up the affair," Frank said quickly, and Joe added, "Slim, we'll do all we can to help your father."

CHAPTER VIII

An Important Discovery

WHEN the Hardy boys were on their way home from school the next afternoon they noticed that a crowd had collected in the vestibule of the post office and were staring at the bulletin board.

"Wonder what's up now?" said Joe, pushing his way forward through the crowd with the agility of an eel. Frank was not slow in following.

On the board was a large poster. The ink on it was scarcely dry. At the top, in enormous black letters, it read:

$1000 REWARD

Underneath, in slightly smaller type, was the following:

The above reward will be paid for information leading to the arrest of the person or persons who broke into Tower Mansion and stole jewels and securities from a safe in the library.

The reward was being offered by Hurd Applegate.

"Why, that must mean the charge against Mr. Robinson has been dropped!" exclaimed Joe.

"It looks like it. Let's see if we can find Slim."

All about them people were commenting on the size of the reward, and there were many expressions of envy for the person who would be fortunate enough to solve the mystery.

"A thousand dollars!" said Frank, as the brothers made their way out of the post office. "That's a lot of money, Joe."

"I'll say it is."

"And there's no reason why we haven't as good a chance of earning it as anyone else."

"I suppose Dad and the police are barred from the reward, for it's their duty to find the thief if they can. But if we track him down we can get the money. It'll be a good sum to add to our college fund."

"Let's go! Say, there's Slim now."

Perry Robinson was coming down the street toward them. He looked much happier than he had the previous evening, and when he saw the Hardy boys his face lighted up.

"Dad is free," he told them. "Thanks to your father, the charge has been dropped."

"I'm sure glad to hear that!" exclaimed Joe. "I see a reward is being offered."

"Your father convinced Mr. Applegate that it

must have been an outside job. And the work of a professional thief. Chief Collig admitted there wasn't much evidence against Dad, so they let him go. It's a great relief. My mother and sisters were almost crazy with worry."

"No wonder," commented Frank. "What's your father going to do now?"

"I don't know," Slim admitted. "Of course, we've had to move from the Tower Mansion estate. Mr. Applegate said that even though the charge had been dropped, he wasn't altogether convinced in his own mind that Dad hadn't had something to do with the theft. So he dismissed him."

"That's tough luck. But your dad will be able to get another job somewhere," Frank said consolingly.

"I'm not so sure about that. People aren't likely to employ a man who's been suspected of stealing. Dad tried two or three places this afternoon, but he was turned down."

The Hardys were silent. They felt very sorry for the Robinsons and were determined to do what they could to help them.

"We've rented a small house just outside the city," Slim went on. "It's cheap and the neighborhood is kind of bad, but we'll have to get along."

Frank and Joe admired Slim. There was no false pride about him. He faced the facts as they came, and made the best of them. "But if Dad doesn't get a job, it will mean that I'll have to go to work full time."

"Why, Slim—you'd have to quit school!" Joe cried out.

"I can't help that. I wouldn't want to, for you know I was trying for a scholarship. But—"

The brothers realized how much it would mean to their chum if he had to leave school. Perry Robinson was an ambitious boy and one of the top ten in his class. He had always wanted to continue his studies and go on to a university, and his teachers had predicted a brilliant career for him as an engineer. Now it seemed that all his ambitions for a high school diploma and a college education would have to be given up because of this misfortune.

Frank put an arm around Slim's shoulders. "Chin up," he said with a warm smile. "Joe and I are going to plug away at this affair until we get to the bottom of it!"

"It's mighty good of you fellows," Slim said gratefully. "I won't forget it in a hurry." He tried to smile, but it was evident that the boy was deeply worried. When he walked away it was not with the light, carefree step which the Hardys associated with him.

"What's the first move, Frank?" Joe asked.

"We'd better get a full description of those jewels. Perhaps the thief tried to pawn them. Let's try all the pawnshops and see what we can find out."

"Good idea, even if the police have already done it." Frank grinned. Then he sobered. "Do you think Applegate will give us a list?"

"We won't have to ask him. Dad should have that information."

"Let's find out right now."

When the boys returned home, they found their father waiting for them. "I have news for you," he said. "Your theory about the wrecked auto being stolen has been confirmed. Collig phoned just now and told me the true ownership had been traced by the engine number. Car belongs to a man over in Thornton."

"Good. That's one more strike against the thief," Joe declared.

But a moment later the boys met with disappointment when they asked their father for a list of the stolen jewels.

"I'm willing to give you all the information I have," said Fenton Hardy, "but I'm afraid it won't be of much use. Furthermore, I'll bet I can tell just what you're going to do."

"What?"

"Make the rounds of the pawnshops to see if any of the jewels have been turned in."

The Hardy boys looked at each other in amazement. "I might have guessed," said Frank.

Their father smiled. "Not an hour after I was called in on the case I had a full description of all those jewels in every pawnshop in the city. More than that, the description has been sent to jewelry firms and pawnshops in other cities near here, and also the New York police. Here's a duplicate list if you want it, but you'll just be wasting time calling at the shops. All the dealers are on the lookout for the jewels."

Mechanically, Frank took the list. "And I thought it was such a bright idea!"

"It *is* a bright idea. But it has been used before. Most jewel robberies are solved in just this manner—by tracing the thief when he tries to get rid of the gems."

"Well," said Joe gloomily, "I guess *that* plan is all shot to pieces. Come on, Frank. We'll think of something else."

"Out for the reward?" asked Mr. Hardy, chuckling.

"Yes. And we'll get it, too!"

"I hope you do. But you can't ask me to help you any more than I've done. It's my case, too, remember. So from now on, you boys and I are rivals!"

"It's a go!"

"More power to you!" Mr. Hardy smiled and returned to his desk.

He had a sheaf of reports from shops and agencies in various parts of the state, through which he had been trying to trace the stolen jewels and securities, but in every case the report was the same. There had been no lead to the gems or the bonds taken from Tower Mansion.

When the boys left their father's study they went outside and sat on the back-porch steps.

"What shall we do now?" asked Joe.

"I don't know. Dad sure took the wind out of our sails that time, didn't he?"

"I'll say he did. But it was just as well. He saved us a lot of trouble."

"Yes, we might have been going around in circles," Frank conceded.

Joe wagged his head. "It looks as if Dad has the inside track on the case—in the city, anyway."

"What have you got in mind?" Joe asked.

"To concentrate on the country. We started out to find the thief because he stole Chet's car. Let's start all over again from that point."

"Meaning?"

"Mr. Red Wig may have come back to the woods expecting to use Chet's car again, and—"

"Frank, you're a genius! You figure the guy may have left a clue by accident."

"Exactly."

Fired with enthusiasm once more, the brothers called to Mrs. Hardy where they were going, then set off on their motorcycles. After parking them at the picnic site, the brothers once more set off for the isolated spot where the jalopy had been hidden.

Everything looked the same as it had before, but Frank and Joe examined the ground carefully for

Frank and Joe examined the circular marks

new footprints. They found none, but Joe pointed out six-inch circular marks at regular intervals.

"They're just the size of a man's stride," he remarked, "and I didn't notice them before."

"I didn't either," said Frank. "Do you suppose that thief tied pads onto his shoes to keep him from making footprints?"

"Let's see where they lead."

The boys followed the circular marks through the thicket. They had not gone far when their eyes lighted up with excitement.

"Another clue!" Joe yelled. "And this time a swell one!"

CHAPTER IX

Rival Detectives

"Maybe," Frank said with a grin, "Dad will take us into his camp when he sees these!"

"*Just* a minute," Joe spoke up. "I thought we were rivals now, and you and I have to solve this mystery alone to earn the reward."

Frank held up a man's battered felt hat and an old jacket. "If these belong to that thief, I think we've earned the money already!"

He felt through the pockets of the jacket, but they were empty. "No clue here," he said.

"This hat has a label, though—New York City store," said Joe.

"And the coat, too," Frank added. "Same shop. Well, one thing is sure. If they do belong to the thief, he never meant to leave them. The labels are a dead giveaway."

"He must have been frightened off," Joe concluded. "Maybe when he found that Chet's jalopy was gone, he felt he'd better scram, and forgot the coat and hat."

"What I'd like to know," Frank said, "is whether some hairs from that red wig may be in the hat."

Joe grinned. "Bright boy." He carried the hat to a spot where the sunlight filtered down through the trees and looked intently at the inside, even turning down the band. "Yowee! Success!" he yelled.

Frank gazed at two short strands of red hair. They looked exactly like those in the wig which the boys had found.

Joe sighed. "I guess we'll *have* to tell Dad about this. He has the wig."

"Right."

Frank and Joe hurried home, clutching their precious clues firmly. Mr. Hardy was still in his study when his sons returned. The detective looked up, frankly surprised to see them home so soon. There was the suspicion of a twinkle in his eyes.

"What! More clues!" he exclaimed. "You're really on the job."

"You bet we have more clues!" cried Frank eagerly. He told the boys' story and laid the hat and jacket on a table. "We're turning these over to you."

"But I thought you two were working on this case as my rivals."

"To tell the truth," said Frank, "we don't know what to do with the clue we've found. It leads to New York City."

Mr. Hardy leaned forward in his desk chair as Frank pointed out the labels and the two strands of red hair.

"And besides," Frank went on, "I guess the only way to prove that the thief owns these clothes is by comparing the hairs in the hat with the red wig. And Joe and I don't have the wig."

With a grin the detective went to his files and brought it out. "Chief Collig left this here."

The strands of hair were compared and matched perfectly!

"You boys have certainly made fine progress," Mr. Hardy praised his sons. He smiled. "And since you have, I'll let you in on a little secret. Chief Collig asked me to see what I could figure out of the wig. He says there's no maker's name on it."

"And there isn't?" Joe asked.

His father's eyes twinkled once more. "I guess Collig's assistants weren't very thorough. At any rate, I discovered there's an inner lining and on that is the maker's name. He's in New York City and I was just thinking about flying there to talk to him. Now you boys have given me a double incentive for going."

Frank and Joe beamed with pleasure, then suddenly their faces clouded.

"What's the matter?" Mr. Hardy asked them.

Joe answered. "It looks as if you're going to solve the case all alone."

"Nothing of the sort," the detective replied. "The person who bought the wig may not have given his name. The hat may have been purchased a long time ago, and it isn't likely that the clerk who sold it will remember who bought it. The same with the jacket."

Frank and Joe brightened. "Then the case is far from solved," Frank said.

"All these are good leads, however," Mr. Hardy said. "There is always the chance that the store may not be far from where the suspect lives. Though it's a slim chance, we can't afford to overlook anything. I'll take these articles to the city and see what I can do. It may mean everything and it may mean nothing. Don't be disappointed if I come back empty-handed. And don't be surprised if I come back with some valuable information."

Mr. Hardy tossed the wig, coat, and hat into a bag that was standing open near his desk. The detective was accustomed to being called away suddenly on strange errands, and he was always prepared to leave at a moment's notice.

"Not much use starting now," he said, glancing at his watch. "But I'll go to the city first thing in the morning. In the meantime, you boys keep your eyes and ears open for more clues. The case isn't over yet by any means."

Mr. Hardy picked up some papers on his desk, as a hint that the interview was over, and the boys left the study. They were in a state of high excitement when they went to bed that night and could not get to sleep.

"That thief must be pretty smart," murmured Joe, after they had talked long into the night.

"The smarter crooks are, the harder they fall," Frank replied. "If this fellow has any kind of a record, it won't take long for Dad to run him down. I've heard Dad say that there is no such thing as a clever crook. If he was really clever, he wouldn't be a crook at all."

"Yes, I guess there's something in that, too. But it shows that we're not up against any amateur. This fellow is a slippery customer."

"He'll have to be mighty slippery from now on. Once Dad has a few clues to work on he never lets up till he gets his man."

"And don't forget *us*," said Joe, yawning. With that the boys fell asleep.

When they went down to breakfast the following morning Frank and Joe learned that their father had left for New York on an early-morning plane. Their mother remarked, "I'll be so relieved when he gets back. So often these missions turn out to be dangerous."

She went on to say that her husband had promised to phone her if he wasn't going to be back by suppertime. Suddenly she added with a tantalizing smile, "Your father said he might have a surprise for you if he remains in New York."

Mrs. Hardy refused to divulge another word. The boys went to school, but all through the morning could scarcely keep their minds on studies. They kept wondering how Fenton Hardy was faring on his quest in New York and what the surprise was.

Slim Robinson was at school that day, but after classes he confided to the Hardys that he was leaving for good.

"It's no use," he said. "Dad can't keep me in school any longer and it's up to me to pitch in and help the family. I'm to start work tomorrow at a supermarket."

"And you wanted to go to college!" exclaimed Frank. "It's a shame!"

"Can't be helped," replied Perry with a grimace. "I consider myself lucky to have stayed in school this long. I'll have to give up all those college plans and settle down in the business world. There's one good thing about it—I'll have a chance to learn supermarket work from the ground up. I'm starting in the receiving department." He smiled. "Perhaps in about fifty years I'll be head of the firm!"

"You'll make good at whatever you tackle," Joe assured him. "But I'm sorry you won't be able to go through college as you planned. Don't give up hope yet, Slim. One never knows what may happen. Perhaps the thief who *did* rob Tower Mansion will be found."

Frank and Joe wanted to tell Slim about the clues they had discovered the previous day, but the same thought came into their minds—that it would be unfair to raise any false hopes. So they said good-by and wished him good luck. Perry tried hard to be cheerful, but his smile was very faint as he turned away from them and walked down the street.

"I sure feel sorry for him," said Frank, as he and Joe started for home. "He was such a hard worker in school and counted so much on going to college."

"We've just *got* to clear up the Tower robbery, that's all there is to it!" declared his brother.

As they neared the Hardy home, the boys' steps quickened. Would they find that their father had returned with the information on the identity of the thief? Or was he still in New York? And were they about to share another of his secrets?

CHAPTER X

A Sleuthing Trip

FRANK and Joe's first stop was the Hardy garage. Looking in, they saw that only Mrs. Hardy's car was there. Their father had taken his sedan to the airport and not brought it back.

"Dad's not home!" Joe cried excitedly. "Now we'll hear what the surprise is." Dashing into the kitchen, he called, "Mother!"

"I'm upstairs, dear," Mrs. Hardy called back.

The boys rushed up the front stairway two steps at a time. Their mother met them at the door of their bedroom. Smiling broadly, she pointed to a packed suitcase on Frank's bed. The boys looked puzzled.

Next, from her dress pocket, Mrs. Hardy brought out two plane tickets and some dollar bills. She handed a ticket and half the money to each of her sons, saying, "Your father wants you to meet him in New York to help him on the case."

Frank and Joe were speechless for a moment,

then they grabbed their mother in a bear hug. "This is super!" Joe exclaimed. "What a surprise!"

Frank looked affectionately at his mother. "You sure were busy today—getting our plane tickets and money. I wish you were going too."

Mrs. Hardy laughed. "When I go to New York for a week end I want to have fun with you boys, not trot around to police stations and thieves' hide-outs!" she teased. "I'll go some other time. Well, let's hurry downstairs. There's a snack ready for you. Then I'll drive my detective sons to the airport."

In less than two hours the boys were on the plane to New York City. Upon landing there, they were met by Mr. Hardy. He took them to his hotel, where he had engaged an adjoining room for them. It was not until the doors were closed that he brought up the subject of the mystery.

"The case has taken an interesting turn, and may involve considerable research. That's why I thought you might help me."

"Tell us what has happened so far," Frank requested eagerly.

Mr. Hardy said that immediately upon arriving in the city he had gone to the office of the company which had manufactured the red wig. After sending in his card to the manager he had been admitted readily.

"That's because the name of Fenton Hardy is

known from the Atlantic to the Pacific!" Joe interjected proudly.

The detective gave his son a wink and went on with the story. " 'Some of our customers in trouble, Mr. Hardy?' the manager asked me when I laid the red wig on his desk.

" 'Not yet,' I said. 'But one of them may be if I can trace the purchaser of this wig.'

"The manager picked it up. He inspected it carefully and frowned. 'We sell mainly to an exclusive theatrical trade. I hope none of the actors has done anything wrong.'

" 'Can you tell me who bought this one?' I asked.

" 'We make wigs only to order,' the manager said. He pressed a button at the side of his desk. A boy came and departed with a written message. 'It may be difficult. This wig is not a new one. In fact, I would say it was fashioned about two years ago.'

" 'A long time. But still—' I encouraged him," the detective went on. "In a few minutes a bespectacled elderly man shuffled into the office in response to the manager's summons.

" 'Kauffman, here,' the manager said, 'is our expert. What he doesn't know about wigs isn't worth knowing.' Then, turning to the old man, he handed him the red wig. 'Remember it, Kauffman?'

"The old man looked at it doubtfully. Then he gazed at the ceiling. 'Red wig—red wig—' he muttered.

" 'About two years old, isn't it?' the manager prompted.

" 'Not quite. Year'n a half, I'd say. Looks like a comedy-character type. Wait'll I think. There ain't been so many of our customers playin' that kind of a part inside a year and a half. Let's see. Let's see.' The old man paced up and down the office, muttering names under his breath. Suddenly he stopped, snapping his fingers.

" 'I have it,' he said. 'It must have been Morley who bought that wig. That's who it was! Harold Morley. He's playin' in Shakespearean repertoire with Hamlin's company. Very fussy about his wigs. Has to have 'em just so. I remember he bought this one, because he came in here about a month ago and ordered another like it.'

" 'Why would he do that?' I asked him.

"Kauffman shrugged his shoulders. 'Ain't none of my business. Lots of actors keep a double set of wigs. Morley's playin' down at the Crescent Theater right now. Call him up.'

" 'I'll go and see him,' I told the men. And that's just what we'll do, Frank and Joe, after a bite of supper."

"You don't think this actor is the thief, do you?" Frank asked in amazement. "How could he have gone back and forth to Bayport so quickly? And isn't he playing here in town every night?"

Mr. Hardy admitted that he too was puzzled. He was certain Morley was not the man who had worn the wig on the day the jalopy was stolen, for the Shakespearean company had been playing a three weeks' run in New York. It was improbable, in any case, that the actor was a thief.

The three Hardys arrived at Mr. Morley's dressing room half an hour before curtain time. Mr. Hardy presented his card to a suspicious doorman at the Crescent, but he and his sons were finally admitted backstage and shown down a brilliantly lighted corridor to the dressing room of Harold Morley. It was a snug place, with pictures on the walls, a potted plant in the window overlooking the alleyway, and a rug on the floor.

Seated before a mirror with electric lights at either side was a stout little man, almost totally bald. He was diligently rubbing creamy stage make-up on his face. He did not turn around, but eyed his visitors in the mirror, casually telling them to sit down. Mr. Hardy took the only chair. The boys squatted on the floor.

"Often heard of you, Mr. Hardy," the actor said in a surprisingly deep voice that had a comical effect in contrast to his diminutive appearance. "Glad to meet you. What kind of call is this? Social —or professional?"

"Professional."

Morley continued rubbing the make-up on his jowls. "Out with it," he said briefly.

"Ever see this wig before?" Mr. Hardy asked

him, laying the hair piece on the make-up table.

Morley turned from the mirror, and an expression of delight crossed his plump countenance. "Well, I'll say I've seen it before!" he declared. "Old Kauffman—the best wigmaker in the country —made this for me about a year and a half ago. Where did you get it? I sure didn't think I'd ever see this red wig again."

"Why?"

"Stolen from me. Some low-down sneak got in here and cleaned out my dressing room one night during the performance. Nerviest thing I ever heard of. Came right in here while I was doing my stuff out front, grabbed my watch and money and a diamond ring I had lying by the mirror, took this wig and a couple of others that were around, and beat it. Nobody saw him come or go. Must have got in by that window."

Morley talked in short, rapid sentences, and there was no mistaking his sincerity.

"All the wigs were red," he stated. "I didn't worry so much about the other wigs, because they were for old plays, but this one was being used right along. Kauffman made it specially for me. I had to get him to make another. But say—where did you find it?"

"Oh, my sons located it during some detective work we're on. The crook left this behind. I was trying to trace him by it."

Morley did not inquire further. "That's all the help I can give you," he said. "The police never did learn who cleaned out my dressing room."

"Too bad. Well, I'll probably get him some other way. Give me a list and description of the articles he took from you. Probably I can trace him through that."

"Glad to," said Morley. He reached into a drawer and drew out a sheet of paper which he handed to the detective. "That's the same list I gave the police when I reported the robbery. Number of the watch, and everything. I didn't bother to mention the wigs. Figured they wouldn't be in any condition to wear if I did get them back."

Mr. Hardy folded the list and put it in his pocket. Morley glanced at his watch, lying face up beside the mirror, and gave an exclamation. "Suffering Sebastopol! Curtain in five minutes and I'm not half made up yet. Excuse me, folks, but I've got to get on my horse. In this business 'I'll be ready in a minute' doesn't go."

He seized a stick of grease paint and feverishly resumed the task of altering his appearance to that of the character he was portraying at that evening's performance. Mr. Hardy and his sons left. They made their way out to the street.

"Not much luck there," Frank commented.

"Except through Mr. Morley's stolen jewelry," his father reminded him. "If that's located in a pawnshop, it may lead to the thief. Well, boys, would you like to go into the theater via the front entrance and see the show?"

"Yes, Dad," the brothers replied, and Joe added, "Tomorrow we'll try to find out the name and address of the thief through his coat and hat?"

"Right," the detective said.

The Hardys enjoyed the performance of *The Merchant of Venice* with Mr. Morley as Launcelot Gobbo, and laughed hilariously at his comedy and gestures.

The next morning the detective and his sons visited the store from which the thief's jacket and hat had been purchased. They were told that the styles were three years out of date and there was no way to tell who had bought them.

"The articles," the head of the men's suit department suggested, "may have been picked up more recently at a secondhand clothing store." The Hardys thanked him and left.

"All this trip for nothing." Joe gave a sigh.

His father laid a hand on the boy's shoulder. "A good detective," he said, "never sighs with discouragement nor becomes impatient. It took years of persistence to solve some famous cases."

He suggested that their next effort be devoted to doing some research in the city's police files. Since Mr. Hardy had formerly been a member of the New York City detective force, he was permitted to search the records at any time.

Frank and Joe accompanied him to headquar-

ters and the work began. First came a run-down on
any known New York criminals who used disguises. Of these men, the Hardys took the reports
on the ones who were thin and of medium height.

Next came a check by telephone on the where-
abouts of these people. All could be accounted for
as working some distance from Bayport at the time
of the thefts, with one exception.

"I'll bet he's our man!" Frank exclaimed. "But
where is he now?"

CHAPTER XI

Anxious Waiting

THE suspect, the Hardys learned, was out of prison on parole. His name was John Jackley, but he was known as Red Jackley because when caught before going to prison he had been wearing a red wig.

"He lives right here in New York, and maybe he's back home by this time," Joe spoke up. "Let's go see him."

"Just a minute," Mr. Hardy said, holding up his hand. "I don't like to leave Mother alone so long. Besides, in this type of sleuthing three detectives together are too noticeable to a crook. This Jackley may or may not be our man. But if he is, he's probably dangerous. I want you boys to take the evening plane home. I'll phone the house the minute the thief is in custody."

"All right, Dad," his sons chorused, though secretly disappointed that they had to leave.

When they reached home, Frank and Joe learned that their mother had been working on the case from a completely different angle. Hers was the humanitarian side.

"I went to call on the Robinsons to try to bolster their spirits," she said. "I told them about your trip to New York and that seemed to cheer them a lot. Monday I'm going to bake a ham and a cake for you to take to them. Mrs. Robinson isn't well and can do little in the kitchen."

"That's swell of you!" Frank said admiringly. "I'll go."

Joe told them he had a tennis match to play. "I'll do the next errand," he promised.

Monday, during a change of classes, Frank met Callie Shaw in the corridor. "Hi!" she said. "What great problem is on Detective Hardy's mind? You look as if you'd lost your best criminal!"

Frank grimaced. "Maybe I have," he said.

He told Callie that he had phoned home at noon confidently expecting to hear that his father had reported the arrest of the real thief of the Applegate money and the exoneration of Mr. Robinson. "But there was no word, Callie, and I'm worried Dad may be in danger."

"I don't blame you," she said. "What do you think has happened?"

"Well, you never can tell when you're dealing with criminals."

"Now, Frank, you're not trying to tell me your

father would let himself get trapped?" Callie said.

"No, I don't think he would, Callie. Maybe Dad hasn't returned because he still hasn't found the man he was looking for."

"Well, I certainly hope that thief is caught," said Callie. "But, Frank, nobody really believes Mr. Robinson did it!"

"Nobody but Hurd Applegate and the men who employ people. Until they find the man who *did* take the stuff, Mr. Robinson is out of a job."

"I'm going over to see the Robinsons soon. Where are they living?"

Frank gave Callie the address. Her eyes widened. "Why, that's in one of the poorest sections of the city! Frank, I had no idea the Robinsons' plight was that bad!"

"It is—and it'll be a lot worse unless Mr. Robinson gets work pretty soon. Slim's earnings aren't enough to take care of the whole family. Say, Callie, how about going over to the Robinsons' with me after school? Mother's sending a ham and a cake."

"I'd love to," Callie agreed. The two parted at the door of the algebra teacher's classroom.

As soon as the last bell had rung, Frank and Callie left the building together. First they stopped at the Shaw house to leave the girl's books.

"I think I'll take some fruit to the Robinsons," Callie said, and quickly filled a bag with oranges, bananas, and grapes.

When the couple reached the Hardy home, Frank asked his mother if any messages had come. "No, not yet," she answered.

Frank said nothing to her about being concerned over his father, as he tucked the ham under one arm and picked up the cakebox. But after he and Callie reached the street, he again confided his concern to Callie.

"It does seem strange you haven't heard anything," she admitted. "But don't forget the old saying, 'No news is good news,' so don't worry."

"I'll take your advice," Frank agreed. "No use wearing a sour look around the Robinsons."

"Or when you're with me, either," Callie said, tossing her head teasingly.

Frank hailed an approaching bus bound for the section of the city in which the Robinsons lived. He and Callie climbed aboard. It was a long ride and the streets became less attractive as they neared the outskirts of Bayport.

"It's a shame, that's what it is!" declared Callie abruptly. "The Robinsons were always accustomed to having everything so nice! And now they have to live here! Oh, I hope your father catches the man who committed that robbery—and soon!"

Her eyes flashed and for a moment she looked so fierce that Frank laughed.

"I suppose you'd like to be the judge and jury at his trial, eh?"

"I'd give him a hundred years in jail!" Callie declared.

When they came to the street where the Robinsons had moved they found that it was an even poorer thoroughfare than they had expected. There were small houses badly in need of paint and repairs. Shabbily dressed children were playing in the roadway.

At the far end of the street stood a small cottage that somehow contrived to look homelike in spite of the surroundings. The picket fence had been repaired and the yard had been cleaned up.

"This is where they live," said Frank.

Callie smiled. "It's the neatest place on the whole street."

Paula and Tessie answered their knock. The twins' faces lighted up with pleasure when they saw who the callers were.

"Frank and Callie!" they exclaimed. "Come in."

The callers were greeted with kindly dignity by Mrs. Robinson. She looked pale and thin but had the same self-possession she had always shown at Tower Mansion.

"We can't stay long," Callie explained. "But Frank and I just thought we'd run out to see how you all are. And we brought something for you."

The fruit, ham, and cake were presented. As the twins ohed and ahed over the food, Mrs. Robinson's eyes filled with tears. "You are dear people," she said. "Frank, tell your mother I can't thank her enough."

Frank grinned as Mrs. Robinson went on, "Callie, we shall enjoy this fruit very much. Many thanks."

Paula said, "It's a wonderful gift. Say, did you know Perry got a better job the second day he was at the supermarket?"

"No. That's swell," Frank replied. "It didn't take the manager long to find out how smart Slim is, eh?"

The twins giggled, but Mrs. Robinson said dolefully, "I wish my husband could find a job. Since no one around here will employ him, he is thinking of going to another city to get work."

"And leave you here?"

"I suppose so. We don't know what to do."

"It's so unfair!" Paula flared up. "My father didn't have a thing to do with that miserable robbery, and yet he has to suffer for it just the same!"

Mrs. Robinson said to Frank hesitantly, "Has Mr. Hardy discovered anything—yet?"

"I don't know," Frank admitted. "We haven't heard from him. He's been in New York following up some clues. But so far there's been no word."

"We hardly dare hope that he'll be able to clear Mr. Robinson," the woman said sorrowfully. "The whole case is so mysterious."

"I've stopped thinking of it," Tessie declared. "If the mystery is cleared up, okay. If it isn't—we won't starve, at any rate, and my father knows *we* believe in him."

"Yes, I suppose it doesn't do much good to keep talking about it," agreed Mrs. Robinson. "We've gone over the whole matter so thoroughly that there is nothing more to say."

So, by tacit consent, the subject was changed and for the rest of their stay Frank and Callie chatted of doings at school. Mrs. Robinson and the girls invited them to remain for supper, but Callie insisted that she must go. As they were leaving, Mrs. Robinson drew Frank to one side.

"Promise me one thing," she said. "Let me know as soon as your father returns—that is, if he has any news."

"I'll do that, Mrs. Robinson," Frank agreed. "I know what this suspense must be like for you and the twins."

"It's terrible. But as long as Fenton Hardy—and his sons—are working on the case, I'm sure it will be straightened out."

Callie and Frank were unusually silent all the way home. They had been profoundly affected by the change that the Tower Mansion mystery had caused in the lives of the Robinsons. Callie lived but a few blocks from the Hardy home, and Frank accompanied her to the door.

"See you tomorrow," he said.

"Yes, Frank. And I hope you'll hear good news from your father."

The boy quickened his steps and ran eagerly into the Hardy house. Joe met him.

"Any phone call?"

Joe shook his head. "Mother's pretty worried that something has happened to Dad."

CHAPTER XII

A Disturbing Absence

ANOTHER whole day went by. When still no word had come from Mr. Hardy, his wife phoned the New York hotel. She was told that the detective had checked out the day before.

Discouraged and nervous about the new mystery of their father's disappearance, Frank and Joe found it almost impossible to concentrate on their studies.

Then, the following morning when Mrs. Hardy came to awaken them, she wore a broad smile. "Your father is home!" she said excitedly. "He's all right but has had a bad time. He's asleep now and will tell you everything after school."

The boys were wild with impatience to learn the outcome of his trip, but they were obliged to curb their curiosity.

"Dad must be mighty tired," Joe remarked, as Mrs. Hardy went downstairs to start breakfast. "I wonder where he came from."

"Probably he was up all night. When he's working on a case, he forgets about sleep. Do you think he found out anything?"

"Hope so, Frank. I wish he'd wake up and tell us. I hate to go back to school without knowing."

But Mr. Hardy had not awakened by the time the boys set out for school, although they lingered until they were in danger of being late. As soon as classes were over, they shattered all records in their race home.

Fenton Hardy was in the living room, and as they rushed in panting, he grinned broadly. He looked refreshed after his long sleep and it was evident that his trip had not been entirely without success, for his manner was cheerful.

"Hello, boys! Sorry I worried you and Mother."

"What luck, Dad?" asked Frank.

"Good and bad. Here's the story: I went to the house where Red Jackley was boarding. Although he seemed to be an exemplary parolee, I decided to watch him a while and try to make friends."

"How could you do that?"

"By taking a room in the same house and pretending to be a fellow criminal."

"Wow!" Joe cried. "And then?"

"Jackley himself spoiled everything. He got mixed up in a jewel robbery and cleared out of the city. Luckily, I heard him packing, and I trailed him. The police were watching for him and he couldn't get out of town by plane or bus. He out-

witted the police by jumping a freight on the railroad."

"And you still followed?"

"I lost him two or three times, but fortunately
I managed to pick up his trail again. He got out of
the city and into upper New York State. Then his
luck failed him. A railroad detective recognized
Jackley and the chase was on. Up to that time I
had been content with just keeping behind him. I
had still hoped to pose as a fellow fugitive and win
his confidence. But when the pursuit started in
earnest, I had to join the officers."

"And they caught Jackley?"

"Not without great difficulty. Jackley, by the
way, was once a railroad man. Strangely enough,
he worked not many miles from here. He managed
to steal a railroad handcar and got away from us.
But he didn't last long, for the handcar jumped
the tracks on a curve and Jackley was badly
smashed up."

"Killed?" Frank asked quickly.

"No. But he's in a hospital right now and the
doctors say he hasn't much of a chance."

"He's under arrest?"

"Oh, yes. He's being held for the jewel thefts
and also for the theft from the actor's dressing
room. But he probably won't live to answer either
charge."

"Didn't you find out anything that would con-
nect him with the Tower robbery?"

"Not a thing."

The boys were disappointed, and their expressions showed it. If Red Jackley died without confessing, the secret of the Tower robbery would die with him. Mr. Robinson might never be cleared. He might be doomed to spend the rest of his life under a cloud, suspected of being a thief.

"Have you talked to Jackley?" Frank asked.

"I didn't have a chance—he wasn't conscious."

"Then you may never be able to get a confession from him."

Fenton Hardy shrugged. "I *may* be able to. If Jackley regains consciousness and knows he's going to die, he may admit everything. I intend to see him in the hospital and ask him about the Tower robbery."

"Is he far away?"

"Albany. I explained my mission to the doctor in charge and he promised to telephone me as soon as it was possible for Jackley to see anyone."

"You say he used to work near here?" Joe asked.

"He was once employed by the railroad, and he knows all the country around here well. Then he became mixed up in some thefts from freight cars, and after he got out of jail, turned professional criminal. I suppose he came back here because he is so familiar with this area."

"I promised to call Mrs. Robinson," Frank spoke up. "Okay to tell her about Jackley?"

"Yes, it may cheer her up. But ask her not to tell anyone."

Frank dialed the number and relayed part of his father's story. The accused man's wife was overwhelmed and relieved by the news, but promised not to divulge the information. Just as Frank finished the call, the doorbell rang. Frank ushered in the private detective Oscar Smuff.

"Your pa home?" he asked.

"Yes. Come in." Frank led the way into the living room.

Smuff, although he considered himself a topnotch sleuth, stood in awe of Fenton Hardy. He cleared his throat nervously.

"Good afternoon, Oscar," said Mr. Hardy pleasantly. "Won't you sit down?"

Detective Smuff eased himself into an armchair, then glanced inquiringly at the two boys. At once Mr. Hardy said, "Unless your business is *very* private, I'd like to have my sons stay."

"Well, I reckon that'll be all right," Smuff conceded. "I hear you're working on this Applegate case."

"Perhaps I am."

"You've been out of town several days," Smuff remarked cannily, "so I deduced you must be workin' on it."

"Very clever of you, Detective Smuff," Mr. Hardy said, smiling at his visitor.

Smuff squirmed uneasily in his chair. "I'm workin' on this case too—I'd like to get that thousand-dollar reward, but I'd share it with you. I was just wonderin' if you'd found any clues."

Mr. Hardy's smile faded. He said, with annoyance, "If I went away, it is my own business. And if I'm working on the Tower robbery, that also is my business. You'll have to find your own clues, Oscar."

"Well, now, don't get on your high horse, Mr. Hardy," the visitor remonstrated. "I'm just anxious to get this affair cleared up and I thought we might work together. I heard you were with the officers what chased this here notorious criminal Red Jackley."

Mr. Hardy gave a perceptible start. He had no idea that news of the capture of Jackley had reached Bayport, much less that his own participation in the chase had become known. The local police must have received the information and somehow Smuff had heard the news.

"What of it?" Mr. Hardy asked in a casual way.

"Did Jackley have anything to do with the Tower case?"

"How should I know?"

"Wasn't that what you were workin' on?"

"As I've told you, that's my affair."

Detective Smuff looked sad. "I guess you just don't want to co-operate with me, Mr. Hardy. I was thinkin' of goin' over to the hospital where this man Jackley is and questionin' him about the case."

Mr. Hardy's lips narrowed into a straight line. "You can't do that, Oscar. He isn't conscious. The doctor won't let you see him."

"I'm goin' to try. Jackley'll come to some time and I want to be on hand. There's a plane at six o'clock, and I aim to leave my house about five-thirty and catch it." He thumped his chest in admiration. "Detectives don't have to show up for a plane till the last minute, eh, Mr. Hardy? Well, I'll have a talk with Jackley tonight. And I may let you know what he says."

"Have it your own way," said Mr. Hardy. "But if you take my advice you'll not visit the hospital. You'll just spoil everything. Jackley will talk when the times comes."

"So there is somethin' in it!" Smuff said triumphantly. "Well, I'm goin' over there and get a confession!" With that he arose, stumped out of the room, and left the house.

CHAPTER XIII

Teamwork

AFTER Smuff left the house, Mr. Hardy sat back with a gesture of despair. "That man," he said, "handles an investigation so clumsily that Red Jackley will close up like a clam if Smuff manages to question him."

At that moment the telephone rang. The boys listened excitedly as Mr. Hardy answered. "Hello. . . . Oh, yes, doctor. . . . Is that so? . . . Jackley will probably live only until morning? . . . I can see him. . . . Fine. . . . Thank you. Good-by."

The detective put back the receiver and turned to the boys. "I'll take that six-o'clock plane to Albany. But if Smuff goes too, it may ruin everything. The Albany police and I must question Jackley first."

"When's the next commercial flight after six?" Joe asked.

"Seven o'clock."

"Then," said Frank, "Smuff can take that one and question Jackley later. Come on, Joe. Let's see what we can do to help Dad!"

"Don't you boys do anything rash," their father warned.

"We won't."

Frank led the way outdoors and started walking down the street.

"What's on your mind?" Joe asked as they reached the corner.

"We must figure out how to keep Detective Smuff in Bayport until seven o'clock."

"But how?"

"I don't know yet, but we'll find a way. We can't have him bursting into that hospital room and spoiling the chance of Dad's getting a confession. Smuff might ruin things so the case will never be solved."

"You're right."

The brothers walked along the street in silence. They realized that the situation was urgent. But though they racked their brains trying to think of a way to prevent Detective Smuff from catching the six-o'clock plane, it seemed hopeless.

"Let's round up our gang," Joe suggested finally. "Perhaps they'll have some ideas."

The Hardys found their friends on the tennis courts of Bayport High.

"Hi, fellows!" called Chet Morton when he saw

Frank and Joe approaching. "You're too late for a game. Where've you been?"

"We had something important to do," Frank replied. "Say, we need your help."

"What's the matter?" asked Tony Prito.

"Oscar Smuff is trying to win that thousand-dollar reward and get himself on the Bayport police force by interfering in one of Dad's cases," Frank explained. "We can't tell you much more than that. But the main thing is, we want to keep him from catching the six-o'clock plane. We—er—don't want him to go until seven."

"What do you want us to do?" Bill Hooper asked.

"Help us figure out how to keep Smuff in Bayport until seven o'clock."

"Without having Chief Collig lock us up?" Jerry Gilroy put in. "Are you serious about this, Frank?"

"Absolutely. If Smuff gets to a certain place before Dad can, the case will be ruined. And I don't mind telling you that it has something to do with Slim Robinson."

Chet Morton whistled. "Oh, ho! I catch on. The Tower business. If that's it, we'll make sure the six-o'clock plane leaves here without that nutty detective." Chet had a special dislike for Smuff, because the man had once reported him for swimming in the bay after hours.

"So our problem," said Phil solemnly, "is to

keep Smuff here and keep out of trouble our-
selves."

"Right."

"Well," Jerry Gilroy said, "let's put our heads
together, fellows, and work out a plan."

A dozen ideas were put forth, each wilder than
the one before. Biff Hooper, with a wide grin, went
so far as to propose kidnaping Smuff, binding him
hand and foot, and setting him adrift in the bay in
an open boat.

"We could rescue him later," he said. The pro-
posal was so ridiculous that the others howled with
laughter.

Phil Cohen suggested setting the detective's
watch back an hour. That plan, as Frank observed,
was a good one except for the minor difficulty of
laying hands on the watch.

"We might send him a warning not to take a
plane before seven o'clock," Tony Prito said, "and
sign it with a skull and crossbones."

"That's a keen idea!" Chet cried enthusiastically. "Let's do it!"

"Wait a minute, fellows," Frank spoke up. "If
Smuff ever found out who wrote it, we'd be up
to our necks in trouble. We could all be arrested!"

"I know!" Joe cried suddenly, snapping his fingers. "Why didn't I think of it before? And it's so
simple, too."

"Well, tell us!" Frank urged.

Joe explained that every once in a while he and Frank went down to Rocco's fruit store to act as clerks while the owner went home to supper. He stayed open evenings until nine.

"Rocco's is only a block from Smuff's house. Smuff knows Frank and I go there, so he wouldn't be surprised to see us in the neighborhood. I suggest that the bunch of us meet casually down near the store and one boy after another stop Smuff to talk. Maybe we can even get him into the shop. You know Smuff loves to eat."

"You can't hate him for that," Chet spoke up. "I'll be glad to invite him in and buy him an apple for his trip."

"A fifteen-minute delay for Smuff is all we need," Frank said.

"I think it's a swell idea," Biff spoke up. "And I'm sure Mr. Rocco will co-operate."

"Who's going to persuade him?" Phil asked.

"That's Frank and Joe's department," Jerry replied.

Rocco was a hard-working man who had come from Italy only a few years ago. He was a simple, genial person and had great admiration for the Hardy boys.

The whole group made their way toward the fruit store, but only the Hardys went inside. The others spread out to watch for Smuff, who was expected to leave his house soon. Each boy went over his part in the plan.

When Frank and Joe walked into the fruit store, they found the dark-eyed Rocco sorting oranges. *"Buona sera,"* he said. "Good evening. How you like my fix the place?"

"Looks swell," Frank answered. "New bins. Better lights." Then he added, "How does your neighbor Smuff like it?"

Rocco threw up his hands in a gesture of disgust. "Oh, that man! He make me mad. He say I charge too much. He tell me I ought to go back to old country."

"Don't pay any attention to him," Joe advised. "Say, Mr. Rocco," he went on, "you look tired. Why don't you go home for an hour or so and let Frank and me take over here?"

"You think I look tired? That worry my wife. Then Rosa say I must close up early." Rocco sighed. "You very kind boys. I do what you say. Come back six-thirty."

As Rocco removed his apron, he said, "I fix trash in yard to burn. You do that?"

"Glad to."

Rocco showed them a wire incinerator in the yard, then left the store. Five minutes later there was a whistle from the street. A signal from Jerry! Frank and Joe went to the front door to watch. Smuff was just backing his car out of the driveway. As prearranged, Phil hurried over and stopped him.

The detective and the boy apparently got into

an argument, but it did not last long enough to satisfy Frank and Joe. The conversation took less than two minutes, then Smuff backed around into the street.

"Hey, Frank," said Joe, "I have an idea. Go light that trash. Make it a roaring fire!"

Without further explanation he dashed into the street, but Frank figured out what was in his brother's mind. He dashed through the store and into the yard. Quickly he lighted the papers in the incinerator in several places. The rubbish blazed lustily.

Joe was intently watching the scene down the street. Smuff was now being "interviewed" by Biff, and Chet came forward to urge Smuff to take some fruit with him on his trip. The detective hesitated, then shook his head and started off in his car.

Only five of the necessary fifteen-minute delay had elapsed! Joe hesitated no longer. Running down the street, he held up one hand for the oncoming car to stop.

"Come quick, Smuff!" he called out. "There's a fire back of Rocco's!"

"Well, you put it out. I'm in a hurry!" the detective told the boy tartly.

"You mean you'd let all of Bayport burn down just because you're in a hurry?" Joe pretended to scoff.

Smuff winced, but still did not move. Joe said,

"Where's the fire?" Smuff cried out

starting back to the store, "Well, Frank and I will have to take care of it alone."

This brought the detective to action. He realized he might be missing a chance to become a hero! In a flash he drove his car down the street and parked in front of the fruit store.

"Where's the fire?" Smuff cried out, nearly bumping into Frank who was dashing from the front door of Rocco's.

"The fire—is—back there—in the yard." Frank pretended to pant. "You go look and see if we ought to turn in an alarm."

Smuff dashed inside the store and hurried to the yard. By this time the Hardys' friends had gathered in Rocco's fruit store. They asked excitedly what was going on.

"Frank! Joe!" yelled Smuff from the rear of the store. "Where's Rocco? Where's a pail? Where's some water?"

CHAPTER XIV

The Confession

"Rocco's not around," Joe replied to Smuff. "There's water in the sink—in the back. Shall I call the fire department?"

"No, I can manage this," Smuff declared. "But where's a pail?"

Frank dashed into the back room and found a pail under the sink. He filled it with water and handed the pail to Smuff, who hurried to the yard. He doused the incinerator flames which hissed and crackled, then died.

"Some people have no sense," Smuff commented. "The idea of anyone starting a fire, then going off and leaving it! I'll bet that was Rocco's work! As for you boys—you had to call me. Didn't have the savvy to put out a simple fire."

"Good thing you were around," Frank observed, suppressing a smile.

"I'll say it was," Smuff agreed. "And Chief Collig is sure goin' to hear about this."

"Oh, please don't tell him about us," Joe spoke up, half closing his eyes so Smuff could not see the twinkle in them.

"I didn't mean that. Oscar Smuff is no squealer. I mean Collig is goin' to hear what *I* did." The detective chuckled. "One more notch in my gun, as the cowboys say."

Suddenly Smuff sobered and looked at his wrist watch. "Oh, no!" he cried out. "Ten minutes to six! I can't make my plane!"

"That's a shame," Frank said consolingly. "But cheer up, Smuff, there's a seven-o'clock plane for Albany. I wish you luck in your interview."

Smuff stormed out of the fruit store and disappeared with his car. The Hardys and their friends burst into roars of laughter which did not stop until a woman customer came into the shop. All the boys but Frank and Joe left.

Rocco returned at six-thirty, pleased that so much fruit had been sold during his absence. "You better salesman than Rocco." He grinned widely.

The Hardys went home, well-satisfied with their day's work. The six-o'clock plane had left without Smuff. Their father could make his trip to the hospital without the annoying detective's interference.

Fenton Hardy did not return home until the

next afternoon. When the boys came from school they found him in high spirits.

"Solved the mystery?" Joe asked eagerly.

"Practically. First of all, Jackley is dead."

"Did he confess?"

"You're not very sympathetic toward the poor fellow, Joe. Yes, he confessed. Fortunately, Oscar Smuff didn't show up while Jackley was talking."

Frank and Joe glanced at each other and their father smiled quietly. "I have an idea," he said, "that you two sleuths know more about this Smuff business than you would care to tell. Well, anyhow, the Albany police and I had a clear field. I saw Jackley before he died and questioned him about the Tower robbery."

"Did he admit everything?"

"Jackley said he came to Bayport with the intention of robbery. He stole a car, smashed it up, and took Chet's. Then he went to rob the ticket office. When he failed in that he decided to hang around town for a few days. He hit upon Tower Mansion as his next effort. Jackley entered the library with gloves on, opened the safe, and took out the jewelry and securities."

"What did he do with the loot?"

"That's what I'm coming to. It was not until Jackley knew he was at the point of death that he did confess to the Tower affair. Then he said, 'Yes, I took the stuff—but I didn't dare try selling any of it right away, so I hid it. You can get all the stuff back easily. It's in the old tower—'

"That was all he said. Jackley lost consciousness then and never regained it."

"When did Smuff get there?" Joe asked eagerly.

"Not until after Jackley had gone into a coma," Mr. Hardy replied. "We both sat by his bed, hoping the man would awaken, but he died within an hour. Just where Jackley hid the loot in the old tower, he was never able to say."

"Does Smuff know what Jackley said?"

"No."

"If the loot's hidden in the old Applegate tower, we'll find it in no time!" Frank exclaimed.

"Tower Mansion has two towers—the old and the new," Joe reminded him.

"We'll search the old tower first."

"The story seems likely enough," Mr. Hardy remarked. "Jackley would gain nothing by lying about it on his deathbed. He probably became panicky after he committed the robbery and hid in the old tower until he was able to get away safely. No doubt he decided to hide the stuff there and take a chance on coming back for it some time after the affair had blown over."

Joe nodded. "That was why Jackley couldn't be traced through the jewels and the bonds. They were never disposed of—they've been lying in the old tower all this time!"

"I tried to get him to tell me in just what part of the tower the loot was hidden," Mr. Hardy continued, "but he died before he could say any more."

"Too bad," said Frank. "But it shouldn't be hard to find the loot, now that we have a general idea where it is. Probably Jackley didn't hide it very carefully. Since the old tower has been unoccupied for a long time, the stuff would be safe there from snoopers."

Joe jumped up from his chair. "I think we ought to get busy and go search the old tower right away. Oh, boy! Maybe we can hand old Mr. Applegate his jewels and bonds this afternoon and clear Mr. Robinson! Let's go!"

"I'll leave it to you boys to make the search," said Mr. Hardy with a smile. "Then you can have the satisfaction of turning over the stolen property to Mr. Applegate. I guess you can get along without me in this case from now on."

"We wouldn't have got very far if it hadn't been for you," Frank declared.

"And I wouldn't have got very far if it hadn't been for you, so we're even." Mr. Hardy's smile broadened. "Well, good luck to you."

As the boys started from the study, Frank said, "Thanks, Dad. I only hope the Applegates don't throw us out when we ask to be allowed to look around inside the old tower."

"Just tell them," his father advised, "that you have a pretty good clue to where the bonds and jewels are hidden and they'll let you search."

Joe grinned. "Frank, we'll have that thousand-dollar reward before the day is over!"

The brothers raced from the house, confident that they were about to solve the Tower Treasure mystery.

CHAPTER XV

The Tower Search

WHEN the Hardy boys reached Tower Mansion at four o'clock the door was opened by Hurd Applegate himself. The tall, stooped gentleman peered at them through his thick-lensed glasses. In one hand he held a sheet of stamps.

"Yes?" he said, seemingly annoyed at being disturbed.

"You remember us, don't you?" Frank asked politely. "We're Mr. Hardy's sons."

"Fenton Hardy, the detective? Oh, yes. Well, what do you want?"

"We'd like to look through the old tower, if you don't mind. We have a clue about the robbery."

"What kind of clue?"

"We have evidence that leads us to believe the jewels and bonds were hidden by the thief in the old tower."

"Oh! You have evidence, have you?" The elderly man peered at the boys closely. "It's that rascal Robinson, I'll warrant, who gave it to you. He hid the stuff, and now he's suggesting where you might find it, just to clear himself."

Frank and Joe had not considered the affair in this light, and they gazed at Mr. Applegate in consternation. At last Joe spoke up.

"Mr. Robinson has nothing to do with this," he said. "The real thief was found. He said the loot was hidden in the old tower. If you will just let us take a look around, we'll find it for you."

"Who was the real thief?"

"We'd rather not tell you, sir, until we find the stolen property, then we'll reveal the whole story."

Mr. Applegate took off his glasses and wiped them with his handkerchief. He stared at the boys suspiciously for a few moments. Then he called out:

"Adelia!"

From the dim interior of the hallway a high feminine voice answered.

"What do you want?"

"Come here a minute."

There was a rustle of skirts, and Adelia Applegate appeared. A faded blond woman of thin features, she was dressed in a fashion of fifteen years before, in which every color of the spectrum fought for supremacy.

"What's the matter?" she demanded. "I can't sit down to do a bit of sewing without you interrupting me, Hurd."

"These boys want to look through the old tower."

"What for? Up to some mischief?"

Frank and Joe feared she would not give her consent. Frank said quietly, "We're doing some work for our dad, the detective Fenton Hardy."

"They think they can find the bonds and jewels in the tower," Hurd Applegate explained.

"Oh, they do, do they?" the woman said icily. "And what would the bonds and jewels be doing in the old tower?"

"We have evidence that they were hidden there after the robbery," Frank told her.

Miss Applegate viewed the boys with obvious suspicion. "As if any thief would be silly enough to hide them right in the house he robbed!" she said in a tone of finality.

"We're just trying to help you," Joe put in courteously.

"Go ahead, then," said Miss Applegate with a sigh. "But even if you tear the old tower to pieces, you won't find anything. It's all foolishness."

Frank and Joe followed Hurd Applegate through the gloomy halls and corridors that led toward the old tower. He said he was inclined to share his sister's opinion that the boys' search would be in vain.

"We'll make a try at it, anyway, Mr. Applegate," Frank said.

"Don't ask me to help you. I've got a bad knee. Anyway, I just received some new stamps this afternoon. You interrupted me when I was sorting them. I must get back to my work."

The man reached a corridor that was heavily covered with dust. It apparently had not been in use for a long time and was bare and unfurnished. At the end was a heavy door. It was unlocked, and when Mr. Applegate opened it, the boys saw a square room. Almost in the center of it rose a flight of wooden stairs with a heavily ornamented balustrade. The stairway twisted and turned to the roof, five floors above. Opening from each floor was a room.

"There you are," Mr. Applegate announced. "Search all you want to. But you won't find anything—of that I'm certain."

With this parting remark he turned and hobbled back along the corridor, the sheet of stamps still in his gnarled hand.

The Hardy boys looked at each other. "Not very encouraging, is he?" Joe remarked.

"He doesn't deserve to get his stuff back," Frank declared flatly, then shrugged. "Let's get up into the tower and start the search."

Frank and Joe first examined the dusty stairs carefully for footprints, but none were to be seen.

"That seems queer," Frank remarked. "If Jackley was here recently you'd think his footprints would still show. Judging by this dust, there hasn't been anyone in the tower for at least a year."

"Perhaps the dust collects more quickly than we think," Joe countered. "Or the wind may get in here and blow it around."

An inspection of the first floor of the old tower revealed that there was no place where the loot could have been hidden except under the stairs. But they found nothing there.

The boys ascended to the next floor, and entered the room to the left of the stair well. It was as drab and bare as the one they had just left. Here again the dust lay thick and the murky windows were almost obscured with cobwebs. There was an atmosphere of age and decay about the entire place, as if it had been abandoned for years.

"Nothing here," said Frank after a quick glance around. "On we go."

They made their way up to the next floor. After searching this room and under the stairway, they had to admit defeat.

The floor above was a duplicate of the first and second. It was bare and cheerless, deep in dust. There was not the slightest sign of a hiding place, or any indication that another human being had been in the tower for a long time.

"Doesn't look very promising, Joe. Still, Jackley may have gone right to the top of the tower."

The search continued without success until the

boys reached the roof. Here a trap door which swung inward led to the top of the tower. Frank unlatched it and pulled on the door. It did not budge.

"I'll help you," Joe offered.

Together the brothers yanked on the stubborn trap door of the old tower. Suddenly it gave way completely, causing both boys to lose their balance. Frank fell backward down the stairway.

Joe, with a cry, toppled over the railing into space!

Frank grabbed a spindle of the balustrade and kept himself from sliding farther down the steps. He had seen Joe's plunge and expected the next moment to hear a sickening thud on the floor five stories below.

"Joe!" he murmured as he pulled himself upright. "Oh, Joe!"

To Frank's amazement, he heard no thud and now looked over the balustrade. His brother was not lying unconscious at the bottom of the tower. Instead, he was clinging to two spindles of the stairway on the floor below.

Frank, heaving a tremendous sigh of relief, ran down and helped pull Joe to the safety of the steps. Both boys sat down to catch their breaths and recover from their falls.

Finally Joe said, "Thanks. For a second I sure thought I was going to end my career as a detective right here!"

"I guess you can also thank our gym teacher for the tricks he taught you on the bars," Frank remarked. "You must have grabbed those spindles with flash-camera speed."

Presently the boys turned their eyes upward. An expression halfway between a grin and a worried frown crossed their faces.

"Mr. Applegate," Joe remarked, "isn't going to like hearing we ruined his trap door."

"No. Let's see if we can put it back in place."

The boys climbed the stairway and examined the damage. They found that the hinges had pulled away from rotted wood. A new piece would have to be put in to hold the door in place.

"Before we go downstairs," said Joe, "let's look out on the roof. We thought maybe the loot was hidden there. Remember?"

Frank and Joe climbed outside to a narrow, rail-inged walk that ran around the four sides of the square tower. There was nothing on it.

"Our only reward for all this work is a good view of Bayport," Frank remarked ruefully.

Below lay the bustling little city, and to the east was Barmet Bay, its waters sparkling in the late afternoon.

"Dad was fooled by Jackley, I guess," Frank said slowly. "There hasn't been anyone in this tower for years."

The boys gazed moodily over the city, then down at the grounds of Tower Mansion. The many roofs of the house itself were far below, and directly across from them rose the heavy bulk of the new tower.

"Do you think Jackley might have meant the *new* tower?" Joe exclaimed suddenly.

"Dad said he specified the old one."

"But he may have been mistaken. Even the new one looks old. Let's ask Mr. Applegate if we may search the new tower, too."

"It's worth trying, anyway. But I'm afraid when we tell him about the trap door, he'll say no."

The brothers went down through the opening. They lifted the door into place, latched it, and then wedged Frank's small pocket notebook into the damaged side. The door held, but Frank and Joe knew that wind or rain would easily dislodge it.

The boys hurried down the steps and through the corridor to the main part of the house.

Adelia Applegate popped her head out of a doorway. "Where's the loot?" she asked.

"We didn't find any," Frank admitted.

The woman sniffed. "I told you so! Such a waste of time!"

"We think now," Joe spoke up, "that the stolen property is probably hidden in the new tower."

"In the new tower!" Miss Applegate cried out. "Absurd! I suppose you'll want to go poking through there now."

"If it wouldn't be too much trouble."

"It *would* be too much trouble, indeed!" she

shrilled. "I shan't have boys rummaging through *my* house on a wild-goose chase like this. You'd better leave at once, and forget all this nonsense."

Her voice had attracted the attention of Hurd Applegate, who came hobbling out of his study.

"Now what's the matter?" he demanded. His sister told him and suddenly his face creased in a triumphant smile. "Aha! So you didn't find anything after all! You thought you'd clear Robinson, but you haven't done it."

"Not yet," Frank answered.

"These boys have the audacity," Miss Applegate broke in, "to want to go looking through the *new* tower."

Hurd Applegate stared at the boys. "Well, they can't do it!" he snapped. "Are you boys trying to make a fool of me?" he asked, shaking a fist at them.

Frank and Joe exchanged glances and nodded at each other. They would have to reveal their reason for thinking the loot was in the new tower.

"Mr. Applegate," Frank began, "the information about where your stolen stuff is hidden came from the man who took the jewels and the bonds. And it wasn't Mr. Robinson."

"What! You mean it was someone else? Has he been caught?"

"He was captured but he's dead now."

"Dead? What happened?" Hurd Applegate asked in excitement.

"His name was Red Jackley and he was a notorious criminal. Dad got on his trail and Jackley tried to escape on a railroad handcar. It smashed up and he was fatally injured," Frank explained.

"Where did you get your information then?" Mr. Applegate asked.

Frank told the whole story, ending with, "We thought Jackley might have made a mistake and that it's the new tower where he hid the loot."

Hurd Applegate rubbed his chin meditatively. It was evident that he was impressed by the boys' story.

"So this fellow Jackley confessed to the robbery, eh?"

"He admitted everything. He had once worked around here and knew the Bayport area well. He had been hanging around the city for several days before the robbery."

"Well," Applegate said slowly, "if he said he hid the stuff in the old tower and it's not there, it must be in the new tower, as you say."

"Will you let us search it?" Joe asked eagerly.

"Yes, and I'll help. I'm just as eager to find the jewels and bonds as you are. Come on, boys!"

Hurd Applegate led the way across the mansion toward a door which opened into the new tower. Now that the man was in a good mood, Frank decided that this was an opportune time to tell him about the trap door. He did so, offering to pay for the repair.

"Oh, that's all right," said Mr. Applegate. "I'll

have it fixed. In fact, Robinson— Oh, I forgot. I'll get a carpenter."

He said no more, but quickened his steps. Frank and Joe grinned. Old Mr. Applegate had not even reprimanded them!

The mansion owner opened the door to the new tower and stepped into a corridor. Frank and Joe, tingling with excitement, followed.

CHAPTER XVI

A Surprise

THE rooms in the new tower had been furnished when it was built. But only on rare occasions when the Applegates had visitors were the rooms occupied, the owner stated.

In the first one Frank, Joe, and Mr. Applegate found nothing, although they looked carefully in closets, bureaus, highboys, and under the large pieces of furniture. They even turned up mattresses and rugs. When they were satisfied that the loot had not been hidden there, they ascended the stairs to the room above. Again their investigation proved fruitless.

Hurd Applegate, being a quick-tempered man, fell back into his old mood. The boys' story had convinced him, but when they had searched the rooms in the tower without success, he showed his disgust.

"It's a hoax!" he snorted. "Adelia was right. I've

been made a fool of! And all because of Robinson!"

"I can't understand it!" Joe burst out. "Jackley said he hid the stuff in the tower."

"If that fellow did hide the jewels and bonds in one of the towers," Applegate surmised, "someone else must have come in and taken them—maybe someone working with him. Or else Robinson found the loot right after the robbery and kept it for himself."

"I'm sure Mr. Robinson wouldn't do that," Joe objected.

"Then where did he get the nine hundred dollars? Explain that. Robinson won't!"

On the way back to the main part of the mansion, Hurd Applegate elaborated on his theory. The fact that the loot had not been found seemed to convince him all over again that Robinson was involved in some way.

"Like as not he was in league with Jackley!" the man stated flatly.

Again Frank and Joe protested that the ex-caretaker did not hobnob with criminals. Nevertheless, the Hardys were puzzled, disappointed, and alarmed. Their search had only resulted in implicating Mr. Robinson more deeply in the mystery.

Back in the hallway of the main house they met Adelia Applegate, who crowed triumphantly when she saw the search party returning empty-handed. "Didn't I tell you?" she cried. "Hurd Applegate, you've let these boys make a fool of you!"

She escorted the Hardys to the front door, while her brother, shaking his head perplexedly, went back to his study.

"We sure messed things up, Frank," Joe declared, as they walked toward their motorcycles. "I feel like a dud rocket."

"Me too."

They hurried home to tell their father the disappointing news. Fenton Hardy was amazed to hear that the stolen valuables had not been located in either tower. "You're sure you went over the place thoroughly?"

"Every inch of it. There wasn't a sign of the loot. From the dust in the old tower, I'd say no one had been there for ages," Frank replied.

"Strange," the detective muttered. "I'm sure Jackley wasn't lying. He had absolutely nothing to gain by deceiving me. 'I hid it in the old tower.' Those were his very words. And what could he mean but the old tower of Tower Mansion? And why should he be so careful to say the *old* tower? Since he was familiar with Bayport, he probably knew that the mansion has two towers, the old and the new."

"Of course, it may be that we *didn't* search thoroughly enough," Joe remarked. "The loot could be hidden under the flooring or behind a movable wall panel. We didn't look there."

"That's the only solution," Mr. Hardy agreed. "I'm still not satisfied that the stolen property isn't

there. I'm going to ask Applegate to permit another search of both towers. And now, I think your
mother wants you to do an errand downtown."

Mrs. Hardy explained what she wanted and
Frank and Joe were soon on their motorcycles
again. When the boys reached the business section
of Bayport they found that Jackley's confession had
already become known. The local radio station had
broadcast it in the afternoon news program and
people everywhere were discussing it.

Detective Smuff walked along the street looking
as if he would bite the head off the first person
who mentioned the case to him. When he saw the
Hardy boys he glowered.

"Well," he grunted, "I hear you got the stuff
back."

"I wish we had," Frank said glumly.

"What!" the detective cried out, brightening at
once. "You didn't get it? I thought they said on the
radio that this fellow Jackley had told your father where he hid it."

"He did. But how did the news leak out?"

"Jackley's door wasn't closed all the time. One
of the other patients who was walking by the room
heard the confession and spilled it. So you didn't
find the loot after all! Ha-ha! That's a good one!
Didn't Jackley say the stuff was hidden in the old
tower? What more do you need?"

"Well, it wasn't there!" Joe retorted hotly.
"Jackley must have made a mistake!"

"*Jackley* made a mistake!" Smuff continued cheerfully. "It looks like the joke's on you fellows and your father!" The would-be sleuth went on down the street, chuckling to himself.

When Frank and Joe returned home they found that Mr. Hardy had been in touch with Hurd Applegate and had convinced him that a more detailed search of the towers would be advisable.

"Boys," he said, "we'll go there directly after supper. I think we'd better not wait until tomorrow."

At seven o'clock the detective and his sons presented themselves at the Tower Mansion. Hurd Applegate met them at the door.

"I'm letting you make this search," he said as he led them toward the old tower, "but I'm convinced you won't find anything. I've talked the case over with Chief Collig. He's inclined to think that Robinson is behind it all and I'm sure he is."

"But how about Jackley's confession?" Mr. Hardy asked him.

"The chief says that could be a blind. Jackley did it to protect Robinson. They were working together."

"I know it looks bad for Robinson," Mr. Hardy admitted, "but I want to give the towers another close examination. I heard Jackley make the confession and I don't believe he was lying."

"Maybe. Maybe. But I'm telling you it was a hoax."

"I'll believe that only if I don't find anything inside or outside either tower," Mr. Hardy declared, his mouth set in a grim line.

"Well, come on, let's get started," Hurd Applegate said, unlocking the door leading to the old tower.

Eagerly the four set to work. They started at the top of the old tower and worked downward. Their investigation left no possibility untouched. All the walls were tapped for hollow sounds which might indicate secret hiding places. The floors were examined closely for signs of any recent disturbance to the wood. But the missing jewels and bonds were not located. Finally the group reached the ground floor again.

"Nothing to do but go on to the new tower," Mr. Hardy commented briefly.

"I'll have to rest and eat something before I do any more," Hurd Applegate said wearily. He led the way to the dining room where sandwiches and milk had been set out. "Help yourselves," he invited. He himself took only crackers and milk when they all sat down.

After the brief stop for refreshment, the Hardys and the mansion owner turned their attention to the new tower. Again they searched carefully. Walls and partitions were tapped and floors were sounded. Every bit of furniture was minutely examined. Not an inch of space escaped the scrutiny of the detective and his helpers.

As the search drew to a close and the loot still had not been found, Mr. Hardy remarked, "It certainly looks as if the stolen property was never hidden here by Jackley. And furthermore, there's no evidence that if he did hide it here, anyone came in to take it away."

"You mean," said Frank, "it's proof that Mr. Robinson did *not* come in here?"

"Exactly."

"Maybe not," Mr. Applegate conceded. "But it still doesn't prove he wasn't in cahoots with the thief!"

"I'm not going to give up this search yet," Mr. Hardy said determinedly. "Perhaps the loot was hidden somewhere outside the old tower."

He explained that it would be difficult to examine the grounds properly at night. "With your permission, Mr. Applegate, my sons and I will return at sunrise tomorrow morning and start work again." As the owner reluctantly nodded his assent, Mr. Hardy turned to Frank and Joe and smiled. "We ought to be able to prove our point before schooltime."

The boys, who had had no time to prepare any homework, reminded their father that a note from him to the principal would be a great help. The detective smiled, and as soon as they reached home he wrote one out, then said good night.

Frank and Joe felt as if their eyes had hardly closed when they opened them again to see their father standing between their beds. "Time to get up if you want to be in on the search," he announced.

The boys blinked sleepily, then sprang out of bed. Showers awakened them fully and they dressed quickly. Mrs. Hardy was in the kitchen when they entered it and breakfast was ready. The sun was just rising over a distant hill.

"Everything hot this morning," Mrs. Hardy said. "It's chilly outside."

The menu included hot applesauce, oatmeal, poached eggs on toast, and cocoa. Breakfast was eaten almost in silence to avoid any delay, and within twenty minutes the three Hardy sleuths were on their way.

"I see you put spades in the car, Dad," Frank remarked. "I take it we're going to do some digging."

"Yes, if we don't locate the loot hidden above ground some place."

When the Hardys reached Tower Mansion they instituted their hunt without notifying the Applegates, who, they were sure, were still asleep. Everything in the vicinity of both towers was scrutinized. Boulders were overturned, the space under the summerhouse examined by flashlight, every stone in the masonry tested to see if it could be dislodged. Not a clue turned up.

"I guess we dig," Frank stated finally.

He chose a bed of perennial bushes at the foot of the old tower where there had been recent planting, and pushed one of the spades in deep with his foot. The tool hit an obstruction. Excitedly Frank shoveled away the dirt around the spot. In half a minute he gave a cry of delight.

"A chest! I've found a buried chest!"

CHAPTER XVII

An Unexpected Find

THROWING out the dirt in great spadefuls, Frank uncovered the chest completely. It was about two feet long, six inches wide, and a foot deep.

"The treasure!" Joe cried out, running up.

Mr. Hardy was at his son's heels and looked in amazement at Frank's discovery. The boy lifted the chest out of the hole and instantly began to raise the lid on which there was no lock.

Everyone held his breath. Had the Hardys really uncovered the jewels and securities stolen from the Applegates? Frank flung back the lid.

The three sleuths stared at the contents. They had never been more surprised in their lives. Finally Joe found his voice.

"Nothing but a lot of flower bulbs!"

The first shock of disappointment over, the detective and his sons burst into laughter. The contents of the chest were such a far cry from what they had expected that now the situation seemed ridiculous.

"Well, one thing is sure," said Frank. "Red Jackley never buried this chest. I wonder who did?"

"I can answer that," a voice behind them replied, and the Hardys turned to see Hurd Applegate, clad in bathrobe and slippers, walking toward them.

"Good morning, Mr. Applegate," the boys chorused, and their father added, "You see we're on the job. For a couple of moments we thought we had found your stolen property."

Hurd Applegate's face took on a stern look. "You didn't find my securities," he said, "but maybe you have found a clue to the thief. Robinson buried that chest full of bulbs. That's what he's done with Adelia's jewelry and my securities! He's buried them some place, but I'd be willing to bet anything it wasn't on the grounds here."

Frank, realizing the man was not in a good humor this morning, tried to steer the conversation away from the stolen valuables. "Mr. Applegate," he said, "why did Mr. Robinson bury these flower bulbs here?"

The owner of Tower Mansion gave a little snort. "That man's nutty about unusual flowers. He sent to Europe for these bulbs. They have to be kept in a cool, dark place for several months, so he decided to bury them. He's always doing something queer like that. Why, do you know what he tried to get me to do? Put up a greenhouse here on the property so he could raise all kinds of rare flowers."

"That sounds like a swell hobby," Joe spoke up.

"Swell nothing!" Mr. Applegate replied. "I guess you don't know how much greenhouses cost. And besides, growing rare flowers takes a lot of time. Robinson had enough to do without fiddling around with making great big daisies out of little wild ones, or turning cowslips into orchids!"

Frank whistled. "If Mr. Robinson can do that, he's a genius!"

"Genius—that's a joke!" said Mr. Applegate. "Well, go on with your digging. I want this mystery cleared up."

It was decided that Mr. Hardy, with his superior powers of observation, would scrutinize the ground near both towers. Wherever it looked as if the ground had been turned over recently, the boys would dig at the spot. The chest of flower bulbs was carefully replaced and the dirt shoveled over it.

"Here's a place where you might dig," Mr. Hardy called presently from the opposite side of the old tower. When the boys arrived with their spades, he said, "I have an idea a dog dug up this spot and probably all you'll find is a beef bone. But we don't want to miss anything."

This time Joe's spade hit the object which had been buried. As his father had prophesied, it proved to be only a bone secreted by some dog.

The three Hardys transferred their work to the new tower. All this time Hurd Applegate had been looking on in silence. From the corners of their eyes, the Hardys could catch an expression of satisfaction on the elderly man's face.

Mr. Hardy glanced at his wrist watch, then said, "Well, boys, I guess this is our last try." He indicated another spot a few feet away. "You fellows must get cleaned up and go to school."

Undaunted by their failures so far, Frank and Joe dug in with a will. In a few moments they had uncovered another small chest.

"Wow, this one is heavy!" Frank said as he lifted it from the hole.

"Then maybe—maybe it's the stolen property!" Joe exclaimed.

Even Mr. Applegate showed keen interest this time and leaned over to raise the lid himself. The box contained several sacks.

"The jewels!" Joe cried out.

"And that flat-shaped sack could contain the securities!" Frank said enthusiastically.

Mr. Applegate picked up one of the circular bags and quickly untied the string wound about the top. His face took on a look of utter disgust. "Seeds!" he fairly shouted.

Mr. Hardy had already picked up the flat sack. He looked almost as disappointed as Mr. Applegate. "Flower catalogs!" he exclaimed. "They seem to be in various foreign languages."

Frank lifted the chest from the hole

"Oh, Robinson was always sending for things from all over the world," the Tower Mansion owner remarked. "I told him to destroy them. He paid too much attention to that stuff when he might have been doing something useful. I suppose he buried the catalogs, so I wouldn't find them."

After a long breath the elderly man went on, "Well, we've reached the end of the line. You Hardys haven't proved a thing, but you've certainly torn up my house and grounds."

The three sleuths had to admit this was true but told him they were still fired by two hopes: to clear Mr. Robinson of the charge against him, and to find the stolen property. As they put their spades back into the Hardy car, Mr. Applegate invited them into the house to wash and have a bite to eat.

"I guess you boys could do with a second breakfast," he added, and the brothers thought, "Maybe at times Mr. Applegate isn't such a bad sort."

They accepted the invitation and enjoyed the meal of waffles and honey. Their father then drove them to Bayport High.

Frank and Joe had no sooner stepped from the car than they heard their names called. Turning, they saw Iola Morton and Callie Shaw coming toward them.

"Hi, boys!"

"Hi, girls!"

"Say, did you hear what happened early this morning?" Callie asked.

"No. School called off for today?" Joe asked eagerly.

"I wish it were." Callie sobered. "It's about Mr. Robinson. He's been arrested again!"

"No!" The Hardys stared at Callie, thunderstruck. "Why?" Frank demanded.

Iola took up the story, saying that she and Chet had heard the bad news on the radio that morning. They had stopped at the Robinsons' home, when their father brought them to school, to find out more about what had happened.

"It seems that Chief Collig has an idea Mr. Robinson was in league with the thief Jackley, that man your father got the confession from. So he arrested him. Poor Mrs. Robinson! She doesn't know what to do."

"And Mr. Robinson had just managed to find another job," Callie said sadly. "Oh, can't you boys do something?"

"We're working on the case as hard as we can," Frank replied, and told the girls about their sleuthing the evening before and early that morning. At that moment the school bell rang and the young people had to separate.

Frank and Joe were deeply concerned by what they had just heard. At lunch they met Jerry, Phil, Tony, and Chet Morton and told them the news.

"This is tough on Slim," Phil remarked.

"Tough on the whole family," Chet declared.

The boys discussed the situation from all angles and racked their brains for some way in which they could help the Robinsons. They concluded that only the actual discovery of the stolen jewels and bonds would clear Mr. Robinson of the suspicion which hung over him.

"That means there's only one thing to do," Frank said. "We *must* find that loot!"

After school he and Joe played baseball for the required period, then went directly home. They had no heart for further sports activities. It was a dull, gloomy day, indicative of rain and this did not raise the boys' spirits.

Frank, who was restless, finally suggested, "Let's take a walk."

"Maybe it'll help clear the cobwebs from our brains," Joe agreed.

They told their mother they would be home by suppertime, then set off. The brothers walked mile after mile, and then, as they turned back, they were drawn as if by magnets to Tower Mansion.

"This place is beginning to haunt me," said Joe, as they walked up the driveway.

Suddenly Frank caught his brother's arm. "I just had an idea. Maybe Jackley in his deathbed confession was confused and meant some other robbery he committed. Besides, at some time in every mystery the most innocent-seeming people become suspect. What proof is there that the Applegates haven't pulled a hoax? For reasons of their own they might say that the things had been stolen from their safe. Don't forget that Dad didn't find any fingerprints on it except Mr. Applegate's."

"Frank, you've got a point there. That man and his sister act so mean sometimes, I wouldn't put it past them to be trying to cheat the insurance company," said Joe.

"Exactly," his brother agreed. "For the moment, let's play it this way. We'll pretend they're suspects and do a little spying about this place."

Instantly the boys left the roadway and disappeared among the shrubbery that lined it. Making their way cautiously, they moved forward toward Tower Mansion. The place was in darkness with the exception of three lighted rooms on the first floor.

"What's your idea, Frank?" his brother whispered. "To learn something that might tell us whether or not the Applegates are implicated in the robbery?"

"Yes. Maybe we'll get a clue if we keep our eyes and ears open."

The boys walked forward in silence. They approached the mansion from the end where the old tower stood. Somewhere, not far from them, they suddenly heard footsteps on the gravel walk. In a flash the brothers dodged behind a tree. The footsteps came closer and the boys waited to see who was approaching. Was it one of the Applegates, or someone else?

Before they could find out, the person's footsteps receded and the boys emerged from their hiding place. Suddenly a glaring light was beamed directly on them.

It came from the top room of the old tower!

CHAPTER XVIII

A Startling Deduction

"Duck!" Frank ordered in a hoarse whisper, quickly dropping to the ground.

Instantly Joe threw himself face down alongside his brother.

"You think the person with the flashlight in the tower saw us?" Frank asked.

"He could have, but maybe not. We sure went down fast."

The strong flashlight was not trained on them again. It was beamed out a window of the tower in another direction, then turned off.

"Well, what say?" Joe asked. "Shall we go on up to the mansion and continue our sleuthing?"

Frank was of the opinion that if they did, they might get into trouble. Even if they had not been recognized, the person in the tower probably had spotted them.

"I'd like to find out who was in the tower," Joe

argued. "It's just possible that the Applegates don't know anything about him."

Frank laughed quietly. "Don't let your imagination run away with you," he advised.

As the boys debated about whether to leave the grounds or to go forward, the matter was suddenly taken out of their hands. From around the corner of the tower rushed a huge police dog, growling and barking. It apparently had scented the brothers and was bounding directly toward them.

Frank and Joe started to run pell-mell, but were unable to keep ahead of the dog. In a few moments he blocked their path menacingly and set up a ferocious barking.

"I guess we're caught," Frank said. "And I hope this old fellow won't take a piece out of my leg."

The two boys tried to make friends with the animal, but he would not let them budge.

"Well, what do we do now?" Joe asked in disgust as the dog continued to growl menacingly.

"Wait to be rescued," Frank replied tersely.

A moment later they saw a bobbing light coming in their direction and presently Mr. Applegate appeared. He looked at the boys in complete astonishment.

"You fellows never give up, do you?" he remarked. "What have you been doing—more digging?"

The brothers did not reply at once. They were embarrassed at having been discovered, but relieved that the man did not suspect what they had really intended to do. The owner of Tower Mansion took their lack of response to mean he was right.

"I'm just not going to have any more of my grounds ruined," he said gruffly. "I've borrowed this watchdog, Rex, and he's going to keep everybody away. If you have any reason for wanting to see me, you'd better phone first, and I'll keep Rex chained."

"Who was up in the tower with a flashlight?" Frank asked the elderly man.

"My sister. She got it into her head that maybe she was smarter than you fellows and could find the stolen stuff in the old tower, but she didn't!" Frank and Joe suppressed grins as he went on. "And then Adelia decided to flash that high-powered flashlight around the grounds, thinking we might have a lot of curious visitors because of the publicity. Apparently she picked you up."

The boys laughed. "Yes, she did," Frank admitted. "Between her and Rex, I guess you needn't worry about any prowlers."

Frank and Joe said good night to Hurd Applegate and started down the driveway. This time the dog did not follow them. He remained at the man's side until the Hardys were out of sight.

As they trudged homeward, Joe remarked, "This seems to be our day for exciting events that fizzle out like wet fireworks."

"Yes. Nothing to show for all our work."

At supper both Mr. and Mrs. Hardy laughed at the boys' story of their encounter with the dog. Then they became serious when Frank asked his father if he thought there was a chance that the Applegates might be guilty of falsely reporting a robbery.

"It's possible, of course," the detective answered. "But the Applegates are so well-to-do I can't see any point in their trying such a thing. I believe it's best for us to stick to the original idea —that someone really did take jewels and securities from the safe, and that the person was Jackley."

As the boys were going to bed that night, Frank remarked to his brother, "Tomorrow is Saturday and we have the whole day free. I vote we set ourselves the goal of solving the mystery before night."

"A big order, but I'm with you," Joe replied with a grin.

They were up early and began to discuss what course of sleuthing they should follow.

"I think we ought to start off on a completely new tack," Joe suggested.

"In which direction?" Frank asked him.

"In the direction of the railroad."

Joe went on to explain that one thing they had not done was find out about Red Jackley's habits when he had worked around Bayport. If they could talk to one or more persons who had known him, they might pick up some new clue which would lead them to the stolen property.

"Good idea, Joe," his brother agreed. "Let's take our lunch and make an all-day trip on our motorcycles."

"Fine."

Mr. Hardy had left the house very early, so his sons did not see him. When his wife heard the boys' plan, she thought it an excellent one and immediately offered to make some sandwiches for them. By the time they were ready to leave she had two small boxes packed with a hearty picnic lunch.

"Good-by and good luck!" Mrs. Hardy called as the brothers rode off.

"Thanks, Mother, for everything!" the young detectives chorused as they started off.

When Frank and Joe reached the Bayport railroad station, they questioned the stationmaster, and learned that he had been with the company only a year and had not known Red Jackley.

"Did he work on a passenger train?" the man asked.

"I don't think so," Frank replied. "I believe he was employed as a maintenance man."

"Then," said the stationmaster, "I'd advise you to go out along the highway to the railroad crossings and interview a couple of old flagmen who are still around. Both of them seem to know everybody and everything connected with the railroad for the past fifty years." He chuckled.

The boys knew of two grade crossings some miles out of town and now headed for them. At the first one they learned that the regular flagman was home ill and his substitute had never heard of Red Jackley. Frank and Joe went on.

At the next crossing they found old Mike Halley, the flagman there, busy at his job. His bright blue eyes searched their faces for a moment, then he amazed them by saying, "You're Frank and Joe Hardy, sons of the famous detective Fenton Hardy."

"You know us?" Frank asked. "I must confess I don't recall having met you before."

"And you ain't," the man responded. "But I make it a rule to memorize every face I see in the newspapers. Never know when there's goin' to be an accident and I might be called on to identify some people."

The boys gulped at this gruesome thought, then Frank asked Halley if he remembered a railroad man named Red Jackley.

"I recollect a man named Jackley, but he wasn't never called Red when I knew him. I reckon he's the same fellow, though. You mean the one that I read went to jail?"

"That's the man!"

"He out of the pen yet?" Mike Halley questioned.

"He died," Joe replied. "Our dad is working on a case that has some connection with Jackley and we're just trying to find out something about him."

"Then what you want to do," said the flagman, "is go down to the Bayport and Coast Line Railroad. That's where Jackley used to work. He was around the station at Cherryville. That ain't so far from here." He pointed in a northerly direction.

"Thanks a million," said Frank. "You've helped us a lot."

The brothers set off on their motorcycles for Cherryville. When they came to the small town, a policeman directed them to the railroad station, which was about a half mile out of town. The station stood in a depression below a new highway, and was reached by a curving road which ran parallel to the tracks for several hundred feet.

The building itself was small, square, and very much in need of paint. A few nearby frame buildings were in a bad state of disrepair. An old wooden water tank, about seventy yards from one side of the station house, sagged precariously. At the same distance on the other side rose another water tank. This one, painted red, was of metal and in much better condition.

Frank and Joe parked their motorcycles and went into the station. A man in his shirt sleeves and wearing a green visor was bustling about behind the ticket window.

"Are you the stationmaster?" Frank called to him.

The man came forward. "I'm Jake—stationmaster, and ticket seller, and baggage slinger, and express handler, and mail carrier, and janitor, and even rice thrower. You name it. I'm your man."

The boys burst into laughter, then Joe said, "If there's anybody here who can tell us what we want to know, I'm sure it's you. But first, what do you mean you're a rice thrower?"

The station agent guffawed. "Well, it don't happen often, but when a bride and groom comes down here to take a train, I just go out, grab some of the rice, and throw it along with everybody else. I reckon if that'll make 'em happy, I want to be part of the proceedin's."

Again the Hardys roared with laughter. Then Frank inquired if the man had known Red Jackley.

"I sure did," Jake replied. "Funny kind of fellow. Work like mad one minute, then loaf on the job the next. One thing about him, he never wanted nobody to give him any orders."

"Did you know that he died recently?" Frank asked.

"No, I didn't," the stationmaster answered. "I'm real sorry to hear that. Jackley wasn't a bad sort when I knew him. Just got to keepin' the wrong kind of company, I guess."

"Can you tell us any particular characteristics he had?" Frank questioned.

Jake scratched his head above his visor. Finally he said, "The thing I remember most about Jackley is that he was a regular monkey. He was nimble as could be, racin' up and down freight-car ladders."

At that moment they heard a train whistle and the man said hurriedly, "Got to leave you now, boys. Come back some other time when I ain't so busy. Got to meet this train."

The Hardys left him and Frank suggested, "Let's eat our lunch and then come back."

They found a little grove of trees beside the railroad tracks and propped their motorcycles against a large tree.

"I'm starved," said Frank, seating himself under the tree and opening his box of lunch.

"Boy, this is good!" Joe exclaimed a moment later as he bit hungrily into a thick roast beef sandwich.

"If Jackley had only stayed with the railroad company," Frank observed as he munched a deviled egg, "it would've been better for everyone."

"He sure caused a lot of trouble before he died," Joe agreed.

"And he's caused a lot more since, the way things have gone. For the Robinsons, especially."

The boys gazed reflectively down the tracks, gleaming in the sun. The rails stretched far into the distance. Only a few hundred feet from the place where they were seated, the Hardys could see both water tanks: the dilapidated, weather-beaten wooden one, with some of the rungs missing from the ladder that led up its side, and the squat, metal tank, perched on spindly legs.

Frank took a bite of his sandwich and chewed it thoughtfully. The sight of the two water towers had given him an idea, but at first it seemed to him too absurd for consideration. He was wondering whether or not he should mention it to his brother.

Then he noticed that Joe, too, was gazing intently down the tracks at the tanks. Joe raised a cooky to his lips absently, attempted a bite, and missed the cooky altogether. Still he continued gazing fixedly in the same direction.

Finally Joe turned and looked at his brother. Both knew that they were thinking the identical thing.

"Two water towers," Frank said in a low but excited tone.

"An old one and a newer one," Joe murmured.

"And Jackley said—"

"He hid the stuff in the old tower."

"He was a railroad man."

"Why not?" Joe shouted, springing to his feet. "Why couldn't it have been this old *water* tower he meant? He used to work around here."

"After all, he didn't say the old tower of Tower Mansion. He just said 'old tower'!"

"Frank, I believe we've stumbled on a terrific clue!" Joe said jubilantly. "It would be the natural thing for Jackley to come to his former haunts after the robbery!"

"Right!" Frank agreed.

"And when he discovered that Chet's jalopy was gone, he probably thought that the police were hot on his trail, so he decided to hide the loot some place he knew—where no one else would suspect. The old water tower! This must be the place!"

CHAPTER XIX

Loot!

Lunch, motorcycles—everything else was forgotten! With wild yells of excitement, Frank and Joe hurried down the embankment which flanked the right of way.

But as they came to a fence that separated the tracks from the grass and weeds that grew along the side, they stopped short. Someone on the highway above was sounding a car horn. Looking up, they recognized the driver.

Smuff!

"Oh, good night!" Joe cried out.

"The last person we want to see right now," Frank said in disgust.

"We'll get rid of him in a hurry," Joe determined.

The boys turned around and climbed back up the embankment. By this time Oscar Smuff had stepped from his car and was walking down to meet the boys.

"Well, I found you," he said.

"You mean you've been looking for us?" Frank asked in astonishment.

The detective grinned. With an ingratiating air he explained to the boys that he had trailed them for miles. He had seen them leave home on their motorcycles, and almost caught up with them at the Bayport station, only to lose them. But the stationmaster had revealed the Hardys' next destination, and the aspiring sleuth had hastened to talk to the flagman, Mike Halley.

"He told me I'd find you here," Smuff said, self-satisfaction evident in his tone.

"But why do you want us?" Joe demanded.

"I've come to make a proposition," Smuff announced. "I've got a swell clue about Jackley and that loot he hid, but I need somebody to help me in the search. How about it, fellows? If old Smuff lets you in on his secret, will you help him?"

Frank and Joe were astounded at this turn of events. Did the man really know something important? Or was he suddenly becoming clever and trying to trick the Hardys into divulging what they knew? One thing the brothers were sure of: they wanted nothing to do with Oscar Smuff until they had searched the old water tower.

"Thanks for the compliment," Frank said. He

grinned. "Joe and I think we're pretty good our-selves. We're glad you do."

"Then you'll work with me?" Smuff asked, his eyes lighting up in anticipation.

"I didn't say yes and I didn't say no," Frank countered. He glanced at Joe, who was standing in back of the detective. Joe shook his head vigor-ously. "Tell you what, Smuff," Frank went on. "When Joe and I get back to Bayport, we'll look you up. We came out here to have a picnic lunch and relax."

Smuff's face fell. But he was not giving up so easily. "When I drove up, I saw you running like mad down the bank. Do you call that relaxing?"

"Oh, when you sit around awhile eating, your legs feel kind of cramped," Joe told him. "Any-way, we have to keep in practice for the Bayport High baseball team."

Smuff looked as if he did not know whether or not he was being kidded. But finally he said, "Okay, fellows. If you'll get in touch with me the first of the week, I can promise you a big surprise. You've proved you can't win the thousand-dollar reward alone, so we may as well each get a share of it. I've already admitted I need help to solve this mystery."

He turned and slowly ambled up the embank-ment to his car. The boys waved good-by to the detective and waited until he was far out of sight and they were sure he would not return. Then Frank and Joe hurried down to the tracks, vaulted the fence, and ran pell-mell toward the old water tower.

"If only we *have* stumbled on the secret!" Frank said enthusiastically.

"It'll clear Mr. Robinson—"

"We will earn the reward by ourselves—"

"Best of all, Dad will be proud of us."

The old water tower reared forlornly alongside the tracks. At close quarters it seemed even more decrepit than from a distance. When the boys glanced at the ladder with its many rungs missing, they wondered if they would be able to ascend to the top on it.

"If Jackley climbed this ladder we can too," said Frank as he stopped, panting, at the bottom. "Let's go!"

He began to scramble up the rotted wood rungs. He had ascended only four of them when there came an alarming *crack!*

"Careful!" Joe cried out from below.

Frank clung to the rung above just as the one beneath him snapped under his weight. He drew himself up and cautiously put his foot on the next rung. This one was firmer and held his weight.

"Hey!" Joe called up. "Don't break all the rungs! I want to come up too!"

Frank continued to climb the ladder as his brother began the ascent. When they came to any place where a rung had broken off, the boys were obliged to haul themselves up by main force. But finally Frank reached the top and waited until Joe was just beneath him.

"There's a trap door up here leading down into the tank," Frank called.

"Well, for Pete's sake, be careful," Joe warned. "We don't want any more accidents with trap doors."

The boys climbed onto the roof of the tower, which swayed under their weight. Both fully realized their peril.

"We can't give up now!" said Frank, and scrambled over the surface of the roof until he reached the trap door. Joe followed. They unlatched and raised the door, then peered down into the recesses of the abandoned water tank. It was about seven feet in depth and twelve in diameter.

Frank lowered himself through the opening, but clung to the rim until he was sure, from feeling around with his feet, that the floor would not break through. "It's okay," he told Joe, who followed his brother inside.

Eagerly the boys peered about the dim interior. The place seemed to be partly filled with rubbish. There was a quantity of old lumber, miscellaneous bits of steel rails, battered tin pails, and crowbars, all piled in helter-skelter fashion. At first glance there was no sign of the Applegates' stolen possessions.

"The jewels and bonds must be here somewhere," Joe declared. "But if Jackley did put the stuff here, he wouldn't have left it right out in the open. It's probably hidden under some of this junk."

Frank pulled out a flashlight and swung it around. In its glow Joe began to hunt frantically, casting aside the old pails and pieces of lumber.

One entire half of the tower was searched without result. Frank turned the flashlight to the far side and noted that a number of boards had been piled up in a rather orderly crisscrossed manner.

"Joe," said Frank, "I'd say these boards hadn't been thrown here accidentally. It sure looks as if somebody had placed them deliberately to hide something underneath."

"You're right."

Like a terrier after a bone, Joe dived toward the pile. Hastily he pulled away the boards.

Revealed in the neat little hiding place lay a bag. It was an ordinary gunny sack, but as Joe dragged it out he felt sure that the search for the Applegate property had come to an end.

"This must be it!" he exulted.

"The Tower treasure!" Frank smothered a whoop of joy.

Joe carried the sack into the light beneath the trap door.

"Hurry up! Open it!" Frank urged.

With trembling fingers Joe began to untie the

cord around the sack. There were many knots, and as Joe worked at them, Frank fidgeted nervously.

"Let me try," he said impatiently.

At last, with both Hardys working on the stubborn knots, the cord was untied and the bag gaped open. Joe plunged one hand into it and withdrew an old-fashioned bracelet of precious stones.

"Jewelry!"

"How about the securities?"

Again Joe groped into the sack. His fingers encountered a bulky packet. When he pulled it out, the boys exclaimed in unison:

"The bonds!"

The bundle of papers, held together by an elastic band, proved to be the securities. The first of the documents was a negotiable bond for one thousand dollars issued by the city of Bayport.

"Mr. Applegate's property!" Frank cried out triumphantly. "Joe, do you realize what this means? We've solved the mystery!"

The brothers looked at each other almost unbelievingly, then each slapped the other on the back. "We did it! We did it!" Joe cried out jubilantly.

Frank grinned. "And without old Smuff," he said.

"Now Mr. Robinson's cleared for sure!" Joe exclaimed. "That's the best part of solving this mystery."

"You're right!"

The boys rejoiced over their discovery for another full minute, then decided to hurry back to Bayport with the precious sack.

"You go down first, Frank," said Joe. "I'll toss the sack to you and then come myself."

He picked up the bag and was about to hoist it to his shoulders when both boys heard a sound on the roof of the tower. They looked up to see an evil-looking, unshaven man peering down at them.

"Halt!" he ordered.

"Who are you?" Frank asked.

"They call me Hobo Johnny," the man replied. "This here is my quarters and anything in it belongs to me. You got no right in my room. You can't take anything away. And t'anks for finding the wad. I never thought to look around."

Joe, taken aback a moment, now said, "You may sleep here, but this is railroad property. You don't own what's in this tower. Now go on down the ladder, so we can leave."

"So you're going to fight, eh?" Hobo Johnny said in an ugly tone. "I'll see about that!"

Without warning the trap door was slammed shut and locked from the outside!

CHAPTER XX

The Escape

"LET us out of here!" Frank shouted at Hobo Johnny.

"You can't get away with this!" Joe yelled.

The man on the water tower roof gave a loud guffaw. "You think I ain't got no brains. Well, I got enough to know when I'm well off. I ain't in no hurry to collect that treasure you found in the tower. A few days from now will be all right for me to sell it."

"A few days from now?" Joe exclaimed, horrified. "By that time we'll be suffocated or die of starvation."

Frank put an arm around his impulsive brother's shoulder. In a low tone he said, "We won't do either, Joe. I don't think it's going to be too hard to get out of here. If not by the trap door, we'll hack our way out through one side of the tank."

Joe calmed down and both boys became silent. This seemed to worry Hobo Johnny, who called down, "What're you guys up to?"

No answer.

"Okay. I'm leaving you now, but I'll be back for that treasure. Don't try any funny stuff or you'll get hurt!"

The man on the roof waited a few moments for an answer. Receiving none, he shuffled across the tower to the ladder.

"I hope he doesn't break all the rungs," said Joe worriedly. "We won't be able to get down."

Again Frank patted his brother on the shoulder. "I noticed an iron pipe running from the top of this tower to the bottom," he said. "If necessary, we can slide down the pipe."

"How long do you think we should wait before trying to break out of here?" Joe asked.

Before replying, Frank pondered the situation. Not knowing anything about Hobo Johnny's habits, he wondered how far away from the tower the man would go. If not far, the boys might find him waiting below and a tough person to handle. Finally, Frank decided that since the tramp had said he would return in an hour, he must be planning to go some distance away, perhaps to get a couple of his hobo friends to come back and help him.

"I'd say that if we leave in fifteen minutes we'll be safe," was Frank's conclusion.

Every second seemed like an hour, but finally when the fifteen minutes were up, the boys lifted a plank and tried to push up the trap door. It would not budge.

"Where do we try next?" Joe questioned.

Frank was examining the seams around the trap door with the flashlight. Presently he pointed out a section where the wood looked completely dried out.

"It shouldn't be too hard to ram a hole here, Joe. Then you can boost me up, so I can reach through and turn the handle on the lock."

Joe picked up a crowbar and jabbed the sharp end between the edge of the trap door and the board next to it. There was a splintering sound. He gave the tool another tremendous push. The seam widened. Now he and Frank together wedged the end of the crowbar up through the opening.

In a few moments they had sprung the two boards far enough apart so that Frank, by standing on Joe's shoulders, could reach his arm through the opening. He found the handle which locked the trap door and turned it. Joe pushed up the door with the plank.

The boys were free!

Frank pulled himself up through the opening and hurried to the edge of the roof. He looked all around below. Hobo Johnny was not in sight; in fact, there was no one to be seen anywhere.

"Clear field ahead!" he announced.

Now the boys began to carry out their original intention of removing the stolen property from the old water tower. Frank went back to the trap door and Joe handed up the sack, then joined his brother on the roof. The older boy went down the ladder quickly and his brother tossed the treasure to him. Joe lost no time in following.

"We'd better get away from here in a hurry!" Frank advised, and both boys sprinted to their motorcycles.

"Let's divide this stuff. It'll be easier to carry," Frank suggested.

He opened the sack and handed Joe the bundle of securities, which the boy jammed into his pocket. Frank stuffed the sack containing the jewelry into his own side pocket. Then they hopped onto their motorcycles, stepped on the starters, and roared down the road toward Bayport. It was not until they were several miles from the old water tower that the Hardys relaxed. Grins spread over their faces.

"I don't know who's going to be the most surprised—Hurd or Adelia Applegate, or Chief Collig or—"

"I have another guess—Dad!" said Frank.

"I guess you're right," Joe agreed. "And the most disappointed person is going to be one Oscar Smuff!"

"What clue do you suppose he wanted us to follow?"

"It's my idea he didn't have any. He just wanted to hook on to us and then claim the glory if we found the treasure, so Collig would give him a job on the force."

"Where do you think we ought to take these valuables?" Joe asked presently.

The boys discussed this as they covered nearly a mile of ground and finally came to the conclusion that since Hurd Applegate had given their father the job of finding the stolen property, the detective should be the one to return it to the owners.

Half an hour later the brothers pulled into the Hardy driveway and soon were overwhelming their parents with the good news.

"It's wonderful! Simply wonderful!" Mrs. Hardy cried out, hugging each of her sons.

Their father's face wore a broad grin. "I'm certainly proud of you," he said, and slapped Frank and Joe on the back. "You boys shall have the honor of making the announcement to the Applegates."

"How about Chief Collig?" Frank asked. "And we'll report Hobo Johnny to him."

"And we'll invite the Robinsons to hear the announcement," Joe added.

The detective said he thought there should be a grand meeting at the Applegates' home of everyone involved with the tower mystery. He suggested that when the boys called up, they try to arrange such a meeting for that very evening.

Frank was selected to make the report to Hurd Applegate; the others could hear the elderly man exclaim in amazement. "I didn't think you'd do it!" he said over and over again.

Shouting for his sister, he relayed the message, then said, "Adelia wants me to tell you she's the most relieved woman in all of Bayport. She never did like any of this business."

The Applegates readily agreed to a meeting at their home early that evening and insisted that Mr. Robinson be there. Mr. Hardy was to see to it that Chief Collig released the man at once.

"This is going to be a lot of fun," Frank declared at supper. "Mother, I think you should come along? Will you?"

"I'd love to," Mrs. Hardy replied. "I'd like to hear what the Applegates and Mr. Robinson and Chief Collig are going to say."

"And Chet should be there too," Joe said. "After all, it was his stolen car that gave us the clue to Red Jackley." Chet was called and gave a whoop of delight. He agreed to meet the Hardy family at the Tower Mansion.

"There's one more person who ought to attend," said Frank with a twinkle in his eye. "Oscar Smuff. I'd like to watch his face, too."

"At least we should tell him that the mystery has been solved," Joe spoke up.

Frank waited until his father had phoned Chief Collig, who promised to release Mr. Robinson at once and bring him out to the Applegates' home. Then Frank called Detective Smuff. He could not resist the temptation to keep Smuff guessing a little longer, and merely invited him to join the conference for a big surprise.

At eight o'clock one car after another arrived at the Tower Mansion. When the Hardy family walked in they found all the Robinsons there. The twins rushed up to Frank and Joe and hugged them. Slim and his father shook the brothers' hands fervently and Mr. Robinson said, "How can I ever thank you?"

There were tears in his wife's eyes and her voice trembled as she added her appreciation for what the Hardy boys had done. "You'll never know what this means to us," she said.

Oscar Smuff was the last to arrive. Instantly he demanded to know what was going on. Frank and Joe had hoped to have a little fun with him, but Tessie and Paula, unable to restrain their enthusiasm, shouted, "Frank and Joe Hardy found the jewelry and the papers! They're real heroes!"

As Frank and Joe reddened in embarrassment, Detective Smuff looked at them disbelievingly. "You!" he almost screamed. "You mean the Hardy boys found the treasure?"

As all the others nodded, Slim spoke up, "This means that my father is completely exonerated."

"But how about that nine hundred dollars?" Smuff demanded suspiciously. "What's the explanation of where your father got that?"

Mr. Robinson straightened up. "I'm sorry," he said, "but I must keep my promise to remain silent about that money."

To everyone's amazement, Adelia Applegate arose and went to stand by the man's side. "*I* will tell you where Robinson got that money," she said dramatically. "At my own suggestion I loaned it to him."

"You!" her brother shouted disbelievingly.

"Yes, this was one time when I didn't ask your advice because I knew you wouldn't agree. I knew Robinson needed the money and I really forced him to borrow it, but made him promise to tell no one where he got it. Then when the robbery took place, I didn't know what to think. I was sick over the whole affair, and I'm very, very glad everything's cleared up."

Miss Applegate's announcement astounded her listeners. Robinson stood up, shook her hand, and said in a shaky voice, "Thank you, Miss Adelia."

Hurd Applegate cleared his throat, then said, "I'd like to make an announcement. Will you all please sit down?"

After everyone had taken seats in the large living room of the mansion, the owner went on, "My sister Adelia and I have been talking things over. This whole robbery business has taught us a great lesson. In the future we're not going to be so standoffish from the residents of Bayport. We're going to dedicate part of our grounds—the part with the pond—as a picnic and swimming spot for the townspeople."

"Super!" exclaimed Chet, and Mrs. Hardy said, "I know everyone will appreciate that."

"I haven't finished," Hurd Applegate went on. "I want to make a public apology to Mr. Robinson. Adelia and I are extremely sorry for all the trouble we've caused him. Robinson, if you will come back and work for us, we promise to treat you like the gentleman you are. We will increase your salary and we have decided to build that greenhouse you want. You'll have free rein to raise all the rare flowers you wish to."

There was a gasp from everyone in the room. All eyes were turned on Mr. Robinson. Slowly he arose from his chair, walked over to Mr. Applegate, and shook his hand.

"No hard feelings," he said. "I'll be happy to have my old position back, and with the new greenhouse, I'm sure I'll win a lot of blue ribbons for you and Miss Adelia."

As he returned to his chair, Mr. Applegate said, "There is just one more item of business—the reward. The thousand-dollar reward goes to Frank and Joe Hardy, who solved the mystery of the Tower treasure."

"A thousand bucks!" exclaimed Detective Smuff.

"Dollars, Mr. Smuff—dollars!" Adelia Applegate corrected him severely. "No slang, please, not in Tower Mansion."

"One thousand iron men," Smuff continued, unheeding. "One thousand round, fat, juicy smackers. For two high school boys! And a real detective like me—"

The thought was too much for him. He dropped his head in his hands and groaned aloud. Frank and Joe did not dare look at each other. They were finding it difficult to restrain their laughter.

"Yes, a thousand dollars," Hurd Applegate went on. "Five hundred to each boy."

He took the two checks from a pocket and handed one each to Frank and Joe, who accepted them with thanks. Mr. Applegate now invited his guests into the dining room for sandwiches, cake, and cold drinks.

As Frank and Joe ate, they were congratulated over and over by the others in the room. They accepted it all with a grin, but secretly, each boy had a little feeling of sadness that the case had ended. They hoped another mystery would soon come their way, and one did at **THE HOUSE ON THE CLIFF.**

"Later, on the way home, Mr. Hardy asked his sons, "What are you fellows going to do with all that money?"

Frank had an instant answer. "Put most of it in the bank."

And Joe added, "Frank and I for some time have wanted to build a crime lab on the second floor of our barn. Now we can do it. All right, Dad?"

The detective smiled and nodded. "An **excellent** idea!"

ORDER FORM

HARDY BOYS MYSTERY SERIES
by Franklin W. Dixon

57 TITLES AT YOUR BOOKSELLER
OR COMPLETE AND MAIL THIS
HANDY COUPON TO:

GROSSET & DUNLAP, INC.
P.O. Box 941, Madison Square Post Office, New York, N.Y. 10010
Please send me the Hardy Boys Mystery and Adventure Book(s) checked
below @ $2.95 each, plus 25¢ *per book* postage and handling. My check or
money order for $_____ is enclosed.

1. Tower Treasure	8901-7	☐ 28. The Sign of the Crooked Arrow 8928-9
2. House on the Cliff	8902-5	☐ 29. The Secret of the Lost Tunnel 8929-7
3. Secret of the Old Mill	8903-3	☐ 30. Wailing Siren Mystery 8930-0
4. Missing Chums	8904-1	☐ 31. Secret of Wildcat Swamp 8931-9
5. Hunting for Hidden Gold	8905-X	☐ 32. Crisscross Shadow 8932-7
6. Shore Road Mystery	8906-8	☐ 33. The Yellow Feather Mystery 8933-5
7. Secret of the Caves	8907-8	☐ 34. The Hooded Hawk Mystery 8934-3
8. Mystery of Cabin Island	8908-4	☐ 35. The Clue in the Embers 8935-1
9. Great Airport Mystery	8909-2	☐ 36. The Secrets of Pirates Hill 8936-X
10. What Happened At Midnight	8910-6	☐ 37. Ghost at Skeleton Rock 8937-8
11. While the Clock Ticked	8911-4	☐ 38. Mystery at Devil's Paw 8938-6
12. Footprints Under the Window	8912-2	☐ 39. Mystery of the Chinese Junk 8939-4
13. Mark on the Door	8913-0	☐ 40. Mystery of the Desert Giant 8940-8
14. Hidden Harbor Mystery	8914-9	☐ 41. Clue of the Screeching Owl 8941-6
15. Sinister Sign Post	8915-7	☐ 42. Viking Symbol Mystery 8942-4
16. A Figure in Hiding	8916-~6	☐ 43. Mystery of the Aztec Warrior 8943-2
17. Secret Warning	8917-3	☐ 44. Haunted Fort 8944-0
18. Twisted Claw	8918-1	☐ 45. Mystery of the Spiral Bridge 8945-9
19. Disappearing Floor	8919-X	☐ 46. Secret Agent on Flight 101 8946-7
20. Mystery of the Flying Express	8920-3	☐ 47. Mystery of the Whale Tattoo 8947-5
21. The Clue of the Broken Blade	8921-1	☐ 48. The Arctic Patrol Mystery 8948-3
22. The Flickering Torch Mystery	8922-X	☐ 49. The Bombay Boomerang 8949-1
23. Melted Coins	8923-8	☐ 50. Danger on Vampire Trail 8950-5
24. Short-Wave Mystery	8924-6	☐ 51. The Masked Monkey 8951-3
25. Secret Panel	8925-4	☐ 52. The Shattered Helmet 8952-3
26. The Phantom Freighter	8926-2	☐ 53. The Clue of the Hissing Serpent 8953-X
27. Secret of Skull Mountain	8927-0	☐ 54. The Mysterious Caravan 8954-8
		☐ 55. The Witchmaster's Key 8955-6
		☐ 56. The Jungle Pyramid 8956-4
		☐ 57. The Firebird Rocket 8957-2

SHIP TO:

NAME _____

(please print)

ADDRESS _____

CITY _____ STATE _____ ZIP _____

Printed in U.S.A.   **Please do not send cash.**